manazuru

manazuru

a novel

Hiromi Kawakami

Translated by Michael Emmerich

COUNTERPOINT

BERKELEY

Library of Congress Cataloging-in-Publication Data

Kawakami, Hiromi, 1958–
[Manazuru. English]
Manazuru / by Hiromi Kawakami ; translated by Michael Emmerich.
    p. cm.
Hardcover ISBN 978-1-58243-627-2
Paperback ISBN 978-1-58243-600-5
1. Abandoned wives—Fiction. 2. Paramours—Family relationships—Fiction. 3. Loss (Psychology)—Fiction. 4. Memory—Fiction. 5. Manazuru-machi (Japan)—Fiction. 6. Psychological fiction. I. Emmerich, Michael. II. Title.

PL855.A859M3613 2010
895.6'35—dc22

2010017806

Cover design by Gopa & Ted2 Inc.
Interior Design by Megan Jones Design
Printed in the United States of America

This book has been selected by the Japanese Literary Publishing Project (JLPP), an initiative of the Agency for Cultural Affairs of Japan.

COUNTERPOINT
1919 Fifth Street
Berkeley, CA 94710

www.counterpointpress.com

Distributed by Publishers Group West

10 9 8 7 6 5 4 3 2 1

one

I WALKED ON, AND something was following. Enough distance lay between us that I couldn't tell if it was male or female. It made no difference, I ignored it, kept walking.

I had set out before noon from the guest house on the inlet, headed for the tip of the cape. I stayed there last night, in that small building set amidst an isolated cluster of private houses, run by a man and woman who, judging from their ages, were mother and son.

It was nearly nine when I arrived, two hours on a train from Tokyo, and by then the entrance to the inn was shut. The entrance was unremarkable: a low swinging iron gate like any other; two or three wiry, gnarled pines; nothing to indicate the lodge's name but a weathered nameplate, ink on wood, bearing the name "SUNA." *Suna* meaning *sand*.

"Unusual name, isn't it?" I asked. "Suna?"

"There are a few in the area," the mother replied.

Her son's hair was graying, though he looked my age, forty-five or so.

When he asked what time I wanted breakfast, it was as if I knew his voice. And yet it was obvious we had never met. Perhaps his voice reminded me of an acquaintance, only I couldn't think who. It wasn't the voice itself, it was a tremor in its depths that I recognized.

I don't need breakfast, I answered, and he emerged from behind the counter to lead the way. My room was at the end of the hall. I'll come back to spread the futon, he announced dryly, the bath is downstairs. When he was gone, I drew the thin curtain aside and saw the sea before me. I could hear the waves. There was no moon. I strained my eyes, peering out into the darkness, trying to make out the waves, without success. The room felt warm, stuffy, as if it had been readied long in advance. I slid the window open and let the cool air flow in.

THE BATH WAS dim. Condensation dripped, slowly, from the ceiling.

I let my thoughts turn to Seiji. I'll have to stay at the office tonight, he'd said. Back in Tokyo. He had described the nap rooms there for me more than once, but I could never picture them in detail. It's just a small, cramped room with a bed, that's all. We have three of them. If the door is locked, you know someone is sleeping inside, he tells me. Never having worked at a company, I picture a hospital room—that's the best I can do. A pipe-frame bed with a beige blanket, enclosed by a curtain; a pair of slippers set out on a floor made of a material that amplifies the sound of footsteps; at the head of the bed, a help button and a temperature chart.

No, it's not like that—just an ordinary, low-ceilinged room. Maybe a magazine lying on the floor that someone left behind. Ordinary. Seiji purses his lips. He never laughs aloud. When he smiles, it shows in his cheeks. This used to puzzle me; now I am used to it.

Whenever I stay in those rooms, he says, by the time I fall asleep, the night is paling. Toward dawn, it grows quiet. Most of the lights are out on every floor, and once it's dark the sounds that echo through the building subside, too. I stretch my exhausted body out on the stiff bed, but I'm so on edge, it's hard to fall asleep—I don't have any rituals for sleeping, not since I was a kid, but when I started spending nights at the office I took up my childhood practice again. I imagine myself floating in water, not half-submerged as I would be in real life, but lying right on the surface, stretched out perfectly still, first the back of my head and then my back, my butt, my heels, resting on the taut surface of the water, motionless, waiting, and as the parts of my body that come in contact with the water begin, little by little, to grow warm, I fall asleep, Seiji says, and once again purses his lips.

I WAS BACK from my bath. Unlike Seiji, there was no need for me to sleep, so I didn't go to bed. Only when the sliver of outside color between the curtains began changing from black to blue did I feel tired. Seiji is probably nodding off right now, I told myself as I switched off the light and closed my eyes.

It was past nine when I woke, and the room brimmed with light. The roar of the waves was louder than the night before. At the front desk, I asked the way to the cape. The son took a pencil and paper and traced the outline of the promontory; then, in the center, he drew in the roads. It looks like something, doesn't it, this shape? I said. Maybe, I don't know. The son's voice reminded me of someone, but still I couldn't think who. I recognized the shape immediately. It was the spitting image of a dragon: the head, from the neck up. Even the whiskers were there, under the nose.

I'd say it's a bit under an hour to the tip on foot, said the son. It'll take longer if you walk slowly, his mother called out from the back room. Oh, and—I haven't made up my mind yet, but I might want to stay tonight, too, if you have a vacancy? I had seen no sign of other guests, I was the only person there last night, I was sure, so I thought I would only have to ask and they would say, Of course, you're welcome to stay. But the son cocked his head, uncertain.

The fishermen come on Fridays. We're usually full up, as long as the waves aren't too choppy. Try giving us a call later. I nodded ambiguously, and left. According to the schedule at the bus stop, the next bus wasn't for half an hour. I wanted to leave my bag at the train station. I could make it to the station in half an hour, even on foot. I peered up the steep incline, wavering, then decided to wait. I went down to the shore.

The ocean is dull. Nothing but waves tumbling in. I sat on a mid-sized rock and stared out over the sea. The wind blew hard. Every now and then a damp burst of spray reached me. The first day of spring had long since come and gone, but the day was chilly. Sand fleas scuttled out from under the rocks, then retreated.

I never planned to come and spend the night here. I had to meet someone at Tokyo Station, we had an early dinner, it was seven when we finished. I was headed for the platform of the

Chūō line when, unbidden, my feet turned and led me instead to the Tōkaidō line, a train came, I got on. I'll go as far as Atami and then turn back, the Chūō Line runs pretty late, it'll be fine, I told myself, and all of a sudden I felt so alone, I endured the loneliness as best I could, and then, unable to bear it, I got off the train. Manazuru was where I disembarked.

I descended from the platform, walked along a narrow corridor, and exited the gate. The station faced a plaza. The information kiosk had been closed for hours. I asked the taxi driver to take me to a guest house. It's small, he told me, but it's a decent place. He let me out in front of the house with the nameplate: "SUNA."

I called Mother from the train. What should I put in Momo's lunch tomorrow? she asked. You can use anything but the chicken in the refrigerator, I started to say, then changed my mind. Use anything, anything at all. I'm sorry, going off all of a sudden, I said. Mother replied, That's all right. Her voice sounded very distant. I had the sense something was following me then, too, and turned to look, but I was alone, standing in the space between two cars, where I had gone to use my cell phone. No sign of anyone, not even a shadow.

I thought I glimpsed the ocean from the train window. In the darkness, I couldn't be sure it was the water, or sure it wasn't. Every so often my work takes me away from home, I leave Mother and Momo alone, together, but I never simply go, without warning, the way I did this time. I don't stay out with Seiji. He has kids of his own. Three kids, and a wife. His middle child is Momo's age. Ninth grade.

I RODE THE bus back to the station, then started out again, on foot, toward the cape.

Surprising, I thought, that they let me stay, without even asking what I was doing there: I had only one small bag with me, and by the time I arrived it was no longer even early evening. I pondered the name on the nameplate, as well. *Suna.* Odd that it didn't strike me last night. It wasn't the sound of the name. It was that I couldn't think of a given name that went well with it.

The road was straight with a gentle incline. Near the port, it began to trace the line of the shore. Each passing car swerved away, giving me a wide berth. Closer to the station there had been people heading in the other direction, but here the street was empty. I approached a cluster of inns and restaurants serving fresh seafood; beyond them there was only the steadily ascending road. In the inns and restaurants, no sign of life.

I did know who the son's voice reminded me of. My missing husband, who disappeared without warning twelve years ago—my husband, as he went to sleep. When drowsiness eddied around him like a haze, straddling that threshold, his voice like a child's. *Kei.* When he said my name, there was sweetness deep in his voice, a hint of moisture, so that for some reason I heard him, beneath the familiar adult male skin, as someone on the cusp of manhood, a boy, or perhaps a young man, it was hard to say which.

My husband vanished, leaving nothing behind. To this day, I have had no news.

I THOUGHT IT might be some spirit of the sea that was following me. My husband loved the sea.

I ignored it, forged on toward the tip of the cape. My breathing deepened. Because I am walking fast, I supposed. The small cloth bag, all I was carrying, swung at my side. I bought a bottle of green tea at a vending machine. I had deliberated briefly whether I wanted it hot or cold, and chose hot. I carried it for a time. Then, just like that, the thing that had been following was gone.

The sky is narrow here, I thought. Perhaps it was the sheerness of the mountain jutting up at my right. A bird was flying, a kite. Flying low. A squat finger of rocks thrust out into the ocean; only there did the kite soar up.

I'm settled now, I think. I don't recall how I lived the first two years after he disappeared. I asked Mother to let us stay with her, accepted any work that came, and gradually I had a life to live. That was when I met Seiji. We became involved almost immediately. What does that mean, anyway? We became involved.

When Momo was born, as she fed at my breast, I thought: She is so close. How close this child and I are. She is closer now, I thought, than when she was inside me. She was not adorable or loveable, that wasn't it. She was close.

To become involved is not to be close. It isn't exactly to be distant, either. When two people become involved, and also when they do not, there is, always, a little separation.

A bus passed by. I was getting tired. The bus stop was only a hundred meters ahead, but I didn't run. The bus drove by without stopping. Another line of seafood restaurants appeared. Seagulls perched on the roofs. Only one restaurant had an OPEN sign hung out, its lights on. Artificial light looks so helpless in the daytime. I went in.

I ORDERED A set lunch. Horse mackerel sashimi.

The fish wasn't minced, as it generally is, but sliced into pieces as large as the ball of my thumb and served with finely chopped ginger and perilla leaves. The mixture was sensuously moist and slightly chewy—the cook must have let the fish marinate in soy sauce for a time. I finished everything: the soup, a fish-bone stock flavored with miso, and a heaping bowl of rice.

I was the only customer. The cook came out and gruffly took my order, then went behind the counter and dished out the soup and the rice. He brought the food to me himself. When he leaned over to set the tray down, I noticed a tear in the sleeve of his white uniform that had been carefully mended.

A wide window looked out on the sea. The kite kept flying in the same pattern as before. Seagulls flew by, too. Earlier I had heard the shrill whistle of their cries and the flapping of their wings; inside, the motion was not accompanied by sound, and the absence unsettled me. It was like watching a silent film.

We went to two silent films at the National Film Center, my husband and I. There was a narrator who read the intertitles that flashed on the screen between each bit of action in a dramatic, sing-song tone. He only did the first movie; there was no narrator for the second.

"I prefer it this way," I said. My husband nodded. Yeah, me too.

Sometimes, of late, I forget him. It's strange, when his presence used to be so thick. When his sudden departure only made his presence thicker.

I THOUGHT IT was rain, but it was spray.

I was on the shore, and the sea was a good ten meters away. A strong wind blew. A chill came over me. When we eat, the heat is drawn away from our hands and feet.

"The blood collects in your stomach," Mother likes to say. Momo's school must be letting out about now. She has only an hour of class on Fridays. She looks just like my husband. Every few years the pendulum swings: first she resembles me, then him. Since she started junior high, she has looked like my husband. The line of her jaw is sharp, her eyes are large. Her complexion is dark.

The tip of the cape wasn't far. Suddenly the incline grew steeper. The cliff was gone, and in its place a wood had appeared. A footpath led deep into it.

Again something was following.

This one is a woman. I've never told anyone about these things that come and follow me. This includes my husband, of course. Today my memory of him is thick. It hasn't been this way for a while. An image of his hometown comes to me. The town was near the Inland Sea. On a mountainside. Each road comes to a dead end near the top, leaving the wind nowhere to go, and in those places, especially, the scent of the tide hangs and eddies.

My husband's mother passed away two years before he disappeared, when Momo was one. His father still lives there, in the same town. We do not see each other.

DID MY HUSBAND want to die?

Or did he disappear because he wanted to live?

Living, dying. Perhaps he had no such thoughts, either way. The trees grew sparse and the pavement widened. The road ended in a roundabout. That must be the bus that passed earlier, waiting at the final stop. The driver was gone. The door was open.

Suddenly the sky opened up. The waves pounded far below. I saw whitecaps shattering. I saw people, one here, there two, descending narrow, twisting paths toward the base of the cliff, where the waves petered out. Figures as small as fingers.

Jump from here, and a second later I'm dead. The thought came, but I cut it off midway. At the words *a second later*. Overcome, not by the impiety of the idea, but by a dull lethargy like the start of a fever. Death is not so distant that I can play with it. Neither, of course, is it so close.

I was still gazing down the cliff when two hikers reached the base. They raised their hands straight overhead, stretching perhaps, and though I could not guess how such tiny, finger-sized people might be feeling, invigorated or sore, the scene was exhilarating. The wind sent the clouds careening, leaving only clear blue above. *Manazuru*. I mouthed the name to feel it in me, then stared for a time at the base of the cliff, and lusted.

I SELDOM LUST for things with a form. Seldom, that is, anymore.

Sometimes it leads to joy, sometimes to a gut-wrenching loneliness, and sometimes it goes nowhere, only hovers, disconnected, lost. I call it lust, wherever it leads. This is nothing more, however, than a name I call it.

The door of the station-bound bus stayed open long after the recorded message announced that the bus was leaving. A man with a child climbed up into it. The child dashed to a seat all the way at the back. The man followed more slowly.

The bus took a road different from the one it had come by. It never filled up. Riders disembarked as new ones boarded, then those who had boarded disembarked. Aside from me, only the man and the child in the last seat rode to the final stop. The plaza in front of the station was full of cars. It seemed odd. Last night, it was so empty.

The child, led by the hand, stepped off the bus. The pair crossed the road at the crosswalk, and the child rapped on the window of a car parked across the way. The back door popped open; the man picked up the child and got in. They live here, maybe. Not just passing through.

I slid a thousand-yen note into the vending machine to purchase a ticket. I never intended to spend a second night. I asked only to hear the answer. Tonight, the woman and man named Suna would welcome crowds of fishermen. The wind was dying down. No sooner had I climbed the steps to the platform than a local train arrived.

"I'M HOME," I said.

Momo sighed ambiguously. That was all.

Lately, she's seemed sullen. She isn't really in a bad mood; at her age, it takes energy to be cheerful. You think she is being sullen when she is simply being.

I brought you a present, I said, holding out a package of squid *shiokara*. She nodded. I had bought it at a stand in the station at Odawara, descending to the gallery below the tracks when I got off the local train to transfer to the express. Momo liked *shiokara* even as a child, despite its intense flavor. Squid fermented in its own salted viscera. My husband liked it, too. I can't say whether or not she takes after him, though, because so do I.

Mother was out shopping. When I opened the door, the house had a subtly different smell. Mother's cooking has a more pungent aroma than mine. What did you have for lunch? I asked. Momo thought for a second, then said, Chicken, it tasted sort of sweet.

I went to my room to change. The gray skirt I had considered wearing then decided against the day before was splayed on the bed where I had thrown it, frozen in the same disarray. I put it on a hanger, hung it in the closet. The air around me loosened. I had only been gone a day, but it takes less than that for the air in an empty room to harden.

When I returned to the living room, Momo had opened a magazine. Maybe I should get a haircut, she mumbled. You'd look nice with short hair, I said. And again she became sullen. We're having hotpot for dinner, she said after a while. When did this happen? When did she stop being so close? She is too close to be distant, now, and too distant to be close.

When she was a newborn, I bathed Momo in a wash basin. For the first month of her life, I never put her in the bathtub, I would clear the table and set a metal basin filled with warm water there, and wash her in the basin.

Opening my left hand, supporting the back of her head with my thumb and middle finger, each turned in to face the other, I uncurled her body face-up in the water. She was so buoyant she floated, almost weightless.

When she was first born her body was scrawny and shriveled, but in the course of her first two weeks she filled out, grew plumper. Deep wrinkles appeared around her ankles, her wrists, her joints. Matter gathered there. New skin formed, and the older layers collected in the wrinkles. One day was all it took: there was more old skin. It was like eraser fuzz. Except for its perfect whiteness. And it had no smell. It kept coming, more and more.

I carefully scrubbed all that off as I bathed her. Momo kept her eyes half shut as I cleaned her body. Sometimes she fell asleep. Only when the time came to wash her head did she begin to wail, wrinkles covering her entire face.

The moment I lifted her from the water, she grew heavy, recovering the weight of her substance. I laid her on the towel I had spread out and rubbed her dry. Then, right away, I opened my blouse and gave her my breast. She seemed thirsty, and gulped as she sucked.

No, loveable was not the word. For a second the heat of her lips repulsed me. I learned then that disgust and tenderness do not stand in opposition. I had never felt such a disgust for the male body. I had thought the male body, my husband's body, was unquestionably necessary. The feeling that welled within me when I held Momo's body was not need, but tenderness.

I COULD NOT fathom Momo's mind. She was just a crying thing. A bud.

I learned a new word: *mushiwarai*, a bug smile. From time to time in its first two weeks of life an infant smiles. But it is not the infant smiling, it is the twitching of the smile bug.

Momo often smiled. Even so, I did not know her mind. I had only just given birth to her, I did not regard her as her own person, she was still my person. Not part of me, not exactly—what I felt was a simple sense of proprietorship. I cannot allow this to be damaged, I thought. It would be an awful waste. I felt tenderness for her. Loveable was not the word.

I felt no desire for the man, my husband. Momo was warmth enough. As long as I suckled her, my body had no desire for my husband. I had no tenderness for him. And yet, in the absence of any tenderness, in my mind I craved him. At night when my husband came to me, I received him willingly with the surface of my body. I had the idea that mind and body were distinct, but the truth is that it is all body. The mind is of the body.

But over time, Momo cooled. She lost her heat, settled into a form. She stopped breastfeeding, she learned to walk, she acquired words.

"Parents' Day is next Wednesday," Momo told me. She was on her way to her room when I walked into the living room, pulling my hair into a ponytail. There was an aroma. The smell of the shampoo she had used last night. Momo's body no longer discards its old skin the way it once did. She has grown cold, solid, marvelously. She carried the scent of her shampoo.

Circle WILL ATTEND and hand it in. Okay. Even as she spoke, Momo was leaving the room. I heard sounds from the front hall.

Mother had returned. The air was shifting. Mother never liked my husband. She didn't say so, but I knew.

As soon as Momo took shape, I began to desire my husband. Just as she stopped suckling. How clever it is, I thought. The body's machinations. I yearned unabashedly for my husband, then felt ashamed. Desire quickly swallowed the shame.

How was Manazuru? Mother trilled, coming into the living room.

IT WAS A strong place, I replied.

Mother gazed at me. Strong? she repeated, trilling again. Then looking me in the eye, she set down her basket of food. A finely woven shopping basket, a flipped trapezoid, short-handled, it bulged from her side when she packed it with vegetables and fish. I used to walk behind Mother as she cradled the basket, wanting her to lead me by the hand, but she wouldn't, and so I walked with my hands behind my back, hiding them. My head didn't even reach her shoulder.

"How many have you gone through?" I asked.

Mother gestured toward the basket, her eyes questioning what I was talking about. "I have no idea," she said. She crooked her fingers, one at a time. The first was before you were born. The next was after you started school. Since then, let's see, I must have worn out two, maybe three.

Who cares if it's ripped, it serves me perfectly well, I don't need another. I won't replace it, she would say, day after day, walking with her torn, misshapen basket. Only when the tears had outgrown mere tears would she give in and grudgingly buy a new one.

Another of the same, please, she would say, proffering the battered basket. The store, run by an aged couple, sold sundry household items. Straw hats, tin hot-water bottles, screws and nails, and shopping baskets. A large S-shaped metal hook hung from a rod that cut across the store, just below the ceiling, and from its tail-like bottom curve two or three baskets dangled.

The same kind, sure thing, hold on a second, the old woman replied. Without a word her husband stood on tiptoe and lifted a basket from the hook. The sunlight has faded it, I'll give you a discount on it. A hundred yen off. I remember her saying that once. The baskets were unadorned, roughly woven, and in the summer the jutting bits of straw would prick your bare arm. You get this same basket every time, don't you? Don't you ever want to try another kind? the old woman asked. I never tire of this one. It's easy to carry, Mother said, and curtly handed her the money.

I go there once in however many years, and every time that woman says the same thing, Mother grumbled when we left the store. There was ice in her voice. I glanced up, surprised, and there was a smile on her face. There was ice in her smile.

Mother took four quarters of a napa cabbage from the basket. Chrysanthemum leaves and shiitake. For a second the air smelled green.

AFTER DINNER THE television came on.

When we had dredged the final strands of udon from the bottom of the earthenware pot, I lifted it, putting a dishrag between the handles and my palms, just in case, though it was no longer too hot to carry with bare hands, and made for the kitchen. The television clicked on.

"It came on by itself!" Momo cried, laughing.

"No one even touched it!" Mother laughed, too.

Seconds later, a noise like the cascading chirp of an alarm clock. It's one of those, Momo said, gesturing toward a row of knobs. A red light glimmered there. It says ALARM, Momo said. She pressed the red light with her fingertip. The chirping stopped. The television stayed on.

It was eight o'clock on the dot. Somehow, without our knowing it, the alarm had been set. Who did it? Momo laughed again. Her laughter is childlike. I set the pot in the sink, turned the faucet on, filled it to the brim. Let it soak, I thought as I turned the faucet off. There are times, when we do a thing, when we think it in words, and there are times when we think it not in words but in pictures, and there are times when we think nothing. Let it soak, I said to myself once again, to see how it felt.

Grandma, Momo asked, did you do it? It wasn't me, Mother answered. Who knew it had an alarm, I had no idea. She takes the television manual from its drawer, puts on her reading glasses, starts reading. I guess it must have been set for eight o'clock when we bought it. It never went off before, though. It's funny, I wonder why, all of a sudden.

The television was still on. A man appeared on the screen, running. The picture cut to a blue sky. Waves surging on the shore. Manazuru. I said the name to myself, watching the man on the screen. The slight hollow of his cheeks made him more handsome. The name Manazuru and the image of the man drift apart without ever having fused. Manazuru. I hadn't repeated the word, but the feeling lingered.

The screen went dark with a click. Momo had the remote control.

MY HUSBAND'S NAME was Rei. I only called him by his family name, Yanagimoto, once. The first time we met, repeating after the person who introduced us, to make sure I had heard correctly. Only that once.

I had trouble calling him by his name at first. I wanted to, I had no choice, but I mumbled. I tried to avoid speaking his name, and my speech grew strained. As if something terrible were sitting right beside me, on one side, and since it wouldn't do to let him see too clearly how I was avoiding it, I struggled to maintain my poise while simultaneously, unconsciously, I shrank, my body pulled away, my motions forced, unnatural—that was the feeling, as my speech unraveled.

"So . . . how was it?"

"What, how was what?"

"Yesterday's event, you said you were going to."

I wanted to ask who had been at a gathering he'd gone to, what they had talked about, but when I couldn't say his name even this simple question died on my lips. Then one day his name exploded from me like a cork from a bottle, and it was no longer a problem. Sometimes, however, even so, it unraveled. Because when I said his name, my mouth grew moist.

He called me Kei right away, very easily. He liked to build things. I hear the sound of him calling me, Kei, his voice, as he saws the wood, wields his hammer, assembles the pieces. The nails sank easily into the rattling board. The hard wood seemed as soft as sand. Sometimes a nail would bend under the powerful blow of the hammer, but the heads always looked new, unblemished, as though they had been pressed in with a soft rubber ball.

"I love how neat the nails are," I said.

Rei smiled. "Say my name," he said suddenly.

R-e-i. I felt jittery saying it. Clasping two nails between his fingers, he leaned forward and pressed his lips to mine. Don't. I drew back, slightly, and Rei's shoulders stiffened. Oh, I thought, then hurriedly spoke his name again. *R-e-i.* The nails dropped from his fingers. He picked them up immediately. The tips are sharp. Wouldn't want you to get hurt. He had his excuse. He gathered the nails, held them to the board, lost himself in their immersion in the wood. He didn't turn to face me again.

His creation became a shelf for Momo's picture books. It is still there, in her room.

I DEBATED WHETHER or not to take down the nameplate: YANAGIMOTO.

Five years had passed since Rei disappeared, and I had admitted to myself that he wouldn't be back. The nameplate became a question.

It was too soon for him to be declared legally dead, but enough time had passed for a divorce. Suddenly I disliked having to live my life in the shadow of my husband's nameplate. Now that we were living with Mother, it hung beside a second nameplate, TOKUNAGA, my maiden name, and I also disliked seeing them there, side by side.

"Are you mad at him?" I asked myself. I was alone. Momo would be in her morning class at elementary school, sitting there in the middle of the classroom, staring blankly at the blackboard; Mother hadn't yet emerged from her room—she takes sleep in little snatches, that is how she is made, sometimes at odd early morning times I would be startled to find her sitting quietly in the kitchen—I sat alone now and asked myself, straight as could be, Are you mad at him?

"Yes, I'm mad." The answer came. I myself, answering myself.

Maybe mad is too strong a word. No, it isn't too strong, if anything it's too weak. I'm mad at Rei. I need, in my anger, to know why he left.

I didn't take down the nameplate. I still go by his name. I am mad, but my anger assumes no form, it is in the cloaked depths, deep in my body's core, that I rage at my husband. The core of me rages, but it also yearns. I have Seiji, but there is something that I can't keep down when I am with him. Rei was the only one. Not just because he was my husband, but because he was the man he was, he was Rei, with him I could keep it down.

Maybe that was why Mother disliked him. Something close made distant, he knew how to carry things, leaving behind no fragments or clippings, his box was the right size, nothing had to be pushed in and no empty spaces remained, he held me ever so easily, he carried me away. I had been so close, and that man, Rei, distanced me, Mother's daughter.

Now that we were living together again, were we close? Three women, our three bodies. Like spheres joined in motion, that is how we are. Not concentric spheres, each sphere cradles its own center, not flat but full, that is how we are.

The nameplate reading TOKUNAGA is hung first. Yanagimoto Momo. It's too hard to say, I'd rather be Tokunaga Momo. I remember Momo saying this. She was laughing. She laughs often. Even now that she is sullen, laughter gushes easily from her.

IT WAS HARD with Rei, but I could call Seiji by his name right away.

Seiji is five years older than Rei, who was two years older than me. Seven years my senior, and we got to know each other through work. I could call him by his name. And softly stroke his shoulder or waist from behind, all of a sudden. Seiji's voice is gentle.

"Ms. Yanagimoto," he calls me. He maintains the same formality. Occasionally he drops from a *yes*, remote as the day we met, to a *yeah*. But he keeps switching back. I am different. I am almost too easy with him.

"Seiji, do me," I say, things like that.

Sometimes he responds, and when he can't he says, "I'm sorry."

That same remoteness.

I was determined to fall for him. When I felt I could love him, I made up my mind to love him. He did not refuse. The current of my feelings flowed his way. This is my loving. The stronger emotions, and the weaker ones, turned and surged, not straight at him, only toward him. I was grateful that he hadn't refused. After Rei's disappearance, I had no place. I didn't know where to channel what I felt. When the path ahead is still unformed, we lose all sense of our location. The fear in me resembled the inability to tell upstream from downstream, to perceive the direction the water was going.

When we do it, he is vocal. Yet he never laughs aloud.

THERE WAS A sign, written vertically, that read INSTRUMENTS & RECORDS.

Head south from the station, walk straight until you come to the sign, then turn left beneath it. The road narrows somewhat, not enough to call it an alley, and then you turn into another street with a soba shop on the corner. There, a few doors down, was the building where Rei lived before we were married.

"What do they call this? An apartment building? A luxury residence?" I asked.

Rei cocked his head. "Do you really have to know?" he asked in return.

No. I was just asking.

INSTRUMENTS & RECORDS. There was a picture of a guitar on the sign. And a round disk, presumably an LP. That store looks kind of old, huh? Have you ever bought a record there? Once again Rei cocked his head. Don't remember. Maybe I did. Or maybe not. Rei was such an easygoing sort. Not a man you expected to disappear. I never imagined it.

I went into INSTRUMENTS & RECORDS once. By myself, on the way to Rei's apartment. Whenever I could find the time, I visited his apartment. Not only when he was there; I went when he wasn't there, too.

"You're a nesting animal, I guess?" Rei asked.

"I've never been like this before," I said, "never."

Rei laughed. He laughed often, just like Momo.

It was brighter inside INSTRUMENTS & RECORDS than I had thought it would be. A popular song was playing—the voice was male. The clerk was a young man. He was about twenty with a long, thin face and long hair, and he was rocking back and forth, to a rhythm different from that of the music playing. There were no other customers.

Flipping through a box of LPs in the "Western Music" section, looking at each one, I was overcome by an urge to go to Rei's apartment. Even though it was practically next door. Even though I would be there in almost no time. Suddenly, I couldn't wait.

There was no reason not to leave empty-handed, but instead I selected an LP at random and hurriedly paid for it. The jacket had a photograph of a woman, in monochrome. I assumed it would be vocal music and that the woman would sing, but it was all instrumental pieces with a neat, driving rhythm. As soon as I stepped into Rei's apartment I tore off the cellophane wrapping and put the record on.

Wow, this is great, Rei said. I like it. So I gave it to him. When we married, I discovered that monochrome jacket among the few dozen records Rei brought with him, and it made me happy. Reunion. I thought the word. *Reunion.* Now that Rei has disappeared, it is hard for me to think it. Inside INSTRUMENTS & RECORDS, everything was faded and warm.

YEAR AFTER YEAR. I can't get used to Parents' Day.

The classroom's dustiness; the samples of calligraphy tacked to the wall, paper curling at the edges; the warmth of the mothers' bodies, and their perfumes; and mixed in, every so often, a father or two, always wearing, for some reason, black or navy blue. It is unfathomable that I, too, once sat day in and day out in a classroom just like this. When I was in junior high, that classroom felt right. In elementary school, that classroom felt right. Maybe because I had nowhere else to go. Or maybe back then I didn't feel this restless burgeoning, this seeping out.

Feeling right was not a matter, then, of thought. Being with Rei felt right almost immediately. So good that I decided to marry him, to let my life become our life. Feeling right is not a help. It is like a mirage. A distant vision, trembling on the sea.

Ill at ease at Parents' Day, I sit in a line with the others, head down. When your turn comes, I'd like each of you to tell me how your children have been lately, any concerns you may have. I'm undecided as to whether or not I should let him have a cell phone. Ever since she entered ninth grade, she's gotten so argumentative, I don't know how to deal with her. He tells me he's always exhausted, he ought to know it's no help to be *too* busy but somehow he can't learn to manage his time. She's been sickly since she was little and she still has to go regularly to the doctor, so for the time being I just want her to build up her strength.

No one says the things they most want to say. This is not a place to say them. Listening to this litany of "how our children have been lately," I lose all sense of how, ordinarily, I engage other people in conversation. I become bewildered.

I went to Parents' Day today, I told Momo when I returned. She gave me a petulant nod. You didn't forget this time. Twice in the past it had slipped my mind. You weren't there today, were you? she asked me the first time, and the second. Before the parents go to talk with the teacher, they sit in on the class. So she could tell right away. She didn't blame me for having skipped it, but it occurred to me that perhaps unconsciously I had been avoiding a place I couldn't grow accustomed to, and I felt ashamed.

"What did you say?"

"That you seem to be enjoying school, you know."

"I wish you wouldn't."

"Sorry."

A sigh escapes me. I take care to keep Momo from hearing. She's that age. I say the words in my mind. She seems so much more confident than me. Confident in her ability to survive her life. Confident because she has no knowledge of what lies beyond the edge.

Or maybe she knows. Maybe her young world contains within it all of life, the way a drop of water holds the universe. What was it like? I can't remember. Your mother really is a dunce. I speak the words aloud. You're a dunce? Momo asks, astonishment written on her face. She comes over, grinning. I love you, Momo. You're such a cutie, such a good girl. My thoughts are in a whirl.

I want to hug her. And yet I hold back. When she was close, I never hesitated. To fold her into my chest, to gather her in.

I forget my fear, and give her a tentative hug.

Laughing, she slides deftly from my arms, away.

COME WITH ME to the department store? Mother asked.

She wanted to send a thank-you gift. I needed to send gifts to two or three people myself, so I agreed without hesitation. At the store, several things came and followed me. One in the thronging basement grocery, near the end of an isle, near the corner. On the side of the escalator where no one was standing, I noticed another.

They are always faint in the department store. Any number of them, faintly fading and then coming back, following and drifting off. Too dim for me to know if they are female or male.

"How would dried shiitake be?" Mother is saying. Dried shiitake? Maybe, I say to keep the conversation going. It is better not to speak too clearly, better to seem unsure, I *wonder* rather than *that's a good idea*—because this is how we keep it going. To acknowledge explicitly that anything is good is a weight on both of us.

We filled out the shipping labels to send a package of dried shiitake to four people, her one, my three. I was writing an address when another thing came. This one was a woman, clearly. Not faint at all, even though we were in a store.

"I'll be back, I'm going to the restroom." Quickly completing the address and handing the labels to Mother, I hurried to the restroom in its out-of-the-way location—invisible, dead space.

The blurry reflection of a woman in the mirror was all it was. Watching it out of the corner of my eye, I stepped into a stall. I was sick to my stomach. I vomited, just a little.

Soon I felt better, and I rinsed my mouth at the sink. I tipped my head back and gargled. The woman stayed. Perhaps she wanted to tell me something. This had never happened before. I had never thrown up before, either. Though I didn't know if she was to blame.

Mother was standing, waiting, when I returned.

"What should we do about lunch, Kei?"

"One of the restaurants upstairs?"

"I feel like having *chirashi-zushi*."

The woman wavered. The air around her bent into darkness for a second, then brightened again, like the flickering of a candle flame. I didn't feel sick again after that. The unpleasantness had already left me, through my mouth. We ascended to the restaurant floor, the woman trailing. Mother ordered eel; I had the *chirashi-zushi*. The restaurants in department stores have such high ceilings. Voices resound. We ate everything, leaving nothing. When we left the store, just like that, the woman was gone.

SOMETIME LATER, THE same woman came and followed me two days straight, so I decided to go again to Manazuru. I had a feeling this woman had been involved, somehow, with Rei.

"I want to go to the beach," Momo said.

So I asked her, "Do you want to go with me?"

And she nodded.

Dress warmly, it's still cool. Okay. The train may rock, you know. Sure.

Momo suffers from motion sickness. It's okay, I've gotten over it now. I have to take the train to school, after all. When Momo announced that she wanted to attend a private school, I worried less about the entrance exam and the tuition than about the daily commute. You're so out of date, Mom, Momo teased.

"Is it for work?" Momo asked.

"No."

"Then why?"

"No particular reason." It's the wrong season for a holiday.

"I wonder if Grandma will come, too?" Momo says happily.

"Grandma says she won't come."

"Why?"

I don't want to go anywhere too strong. That's what Mother had said. Strong places wear me out. You two go on, by yourselves. She was saying no, and yet she spoke the words as though she were singing. Mother is close, I thought. This is how it is, three female bodies, singing, laughing, something unknown that comes and follows, here in this house.

Manazuru, I've never been there before. Momo smiles. It was my first time, too, the other day. We smile together. For a second, I recall how, when the sky suddenly opened out at the tip of the cape and I gazed down at the ocean below, the wind had teased my cheeks, my ears.

two

THERE'S NO NOISE from the tracks, is there? Momo said.
Noise from the tracks? I asked. Then Momo tilted her head
and answered, very quietly, *Tatan tatan. Tatan tatan.*

With that she turned and looked out the window. We sat
in diagonally facing seats, having left Tokyo Station before
noon. Momo was inside, I was near the aisle. She was right,
we couldn't hear the pulsing rattle of the heavy iron car. The
air brimmed with noise, but nothing emerged, no clear-cut
rhythmic line that the human ear might hear as sound. I felt as
though the carriage were simply hovering, my body within it,
in a raucous place.

I wasn't exactly looking at Momo's neck. So thin. Still, years
have passed since it outgrew the alarming thinness of her first
years, when it seemed the slightest pressure would snap it.

Tea? I asked, aligning two small plastic bottles on the windowsill. Momo took one, then immediately put it back. I twisted
off the cap of the other and drank. The liquid coursed down my
throat. It felt cool and good. You should have some, I suggested,
and again she took the bottle in her hand. Indecision. No, I'll
wait, she said, and gave the bottle a small shake. Bubbles rose.

Don't play, I scolded, taking the tone I would use with a small
child. I'm not playing. There is an edge in her voice. The edge cuts

unexpectedly deep. Momo has no intimation of this, of my hurt.
She is simply on edge. It is just a reply, automatic.

Only Momo can wound me like this. She is merciless. She
presses, unconcerned, into the softest places. Ignorant of the oozing pus, the scars. Because with her, I can reveal only the softness.
The parts of me I ought to cover, crust over, protect. I remember
how, very long ago, she was of my body, and I am unable to raise
a barrier, rebuff.

"A BEACHSIDE RESORT hotel," Momo says aloud.

"*Resort*. Kind of makes you blush, doesn't it?" When I
grinned, she grinned.

I wouldn't stay with Momo in the guest house with the
"SUNA" nameplate. The woman and man who ran it, mother and
son, I thought, exuded too adult an atmosphere—I was unwilling
to spend the night there with a child. I worried that it might over-
whelm the boundaries of our togetherness, her and me.

The beachside resort hotel was recommended to us at the
information kiosk. Are we really going here? Momo peered at the
photograph. Such an innocent expression. The woman in the kiosk was talking on the phone with the hotel. Momo went outside.
There was a whitish sky. The temperature wasn't that cool. Tokyo
was bone-chillingly cold. Yes, it's warmer by the sea. There are
plum trees blooming everywhere, the woman in the kiosk says.
Just one night, right? You can check in whenever you like.

Let's go to the seaside, Momo says, her feet picking up into
a dance.

This whole place is the seaside.

I haven't been to the beach in ages.

The three of us used to go to the shore. Rei and Momo and I. Every year, without fail. She and I kept going even after he disappeared, until she turned ten.

The first time, Momo was just over three months old, an infant with a lolling head, and the instant we strode out onto the sand I was seized with fear. It was all right as long as I told myself I was nothing but my own body, but when I let my feelings shift toward Momo's infant weight in my hands, I became terribly afraid.

All this was too intense for a baby. The wind, the tide, the crashing waves. I leaned over Momo, sheltering her. She began to wail. What are you doing that for, can't you see she's hot, she's crying, Rei said.

It's so obvious. It frightens her. Of course she's crying. And yet Rei had no understanding of this. He chattered to Momo. Look, see how big the ocean is! I'm going home. Now. Rei was taken aback when I insisted. Startled to the core.

In the end, we cowered for an hour, as though in hiding, in the beach house, and then left. What a strange person you are, Kei. On the train back, Rei chuckled to himself, several times. Momo was sound asleep. Mother scolded me later. What were you thinking, taking an infant to a place like that, with such strong sunlight! She hasn't even begun to teethe! The next year, around the same time, we went to the beach again. We three. By then, I was no longer afraid.

IT BEGAN TO rain. Sudden gusts of wind.

This sucks, huh. No point being at the seaside with weather like this. Momo nudged closer. Beyond the expanse of glass, we could see the ocean. The choppy waves. A small terrace jutted out beyond the building, two white plastic chairs. Look, Mom, it really is a resort. Momo pointed. The chairs were drenched.

Together we pressed our faces to the window and looked at the rain. Momo's body was warm. Her breath came rapidly. Poor thing, I thought. Pity the young. Pity those who don't know. Not that knowing, or maturity, frees us from pity. But it lessens.

Together we stretched out on the bed and read the hotel guide. They've got a fancy dinner. The word *fancy* is tinctured with laughter. What do you say, should we enjoy a fancy dinner at our beachside resort? Yeah, let's! It's expensive, you know. Are you short on cash, Mom?

The rain beats down, driven by the wind. So far nothing has come and followed me, even though we are in Manazuru. Our room is bright, very clean. In one of the deep drawers in the built-in chest, I discover two white robes, two pairs of white pajamas. Before long Momo is trying on a robe, putting it on over her clothes. It feels lumpy, she says, peeling it off; she starts removing her clothes as well. Once she is down to a T-shirt and underwear, she puts the robe back on. She sits at the edge of her chair and slouches against the backrest, folds her arms behind her head, stares at the ceiling.

"I always wanted to wear a robe," she says, sitting up and fiddling with the pile at the hem.

I recollect the smell of the hospital. Because the room is so bright, perhaps. The smell of the private room where they put my father after his heart attack, when they moved him, for the time being, out of intensive care. I was struck by the hospital's brightness, and by its silence. In bed, my father was hardly there. We took off the gown they had given him in intensive care and helped him into his own pajamas. Mother, the nurse, and I, trying to be gentle as we changed his clothes. He was conscious now, but kept his eyes shut tight. Tubes ran into his mouth and nose. The first time he went to the hospital, he was discharged, after a while; the next year, after his second heart attack, he wasn't.

"It looks good on you," I said, and Momo smirked, wrinkling her nose.

"Don't worry, I've got enough cash for our fancy dinner."

"Great."

"When the rain lets up, we can go outside."

"Do you think it will stop?"

"It will stop, eventually."

"Eventually—"

She broke off, toying again with the hem of her robe.

IT STOPPED AS suddenly as it had begun.

After a rain, the scent of the grass is deeper. Young grass, not even high enough to count as undergrowth, grass like the fuzz on a baby's skin, exuding its smell. We went out for a walk, circled back. Momo slung the strap of her small bag diagonally across her shoulder. The gusts had not stopped blowing. Our hair was whipping about. Momo took out a clip, gathered her hair, fixed it with a sharp snap. A stray strand fell across her forehead.

"Did Dad—"

"Did Dad what?"

The sand over the beach was darkly wet. We spread handker-chiefs on a boulder and sat down, side by side.

"Did Dad smoke?"

"Occasionally." I had to think before I replied. I couldn't remember.

Momo didn't ask anything else. Around the time I first considered taking down our nameplate, it became possible to speak about Rei. Until then, I acted as though nothing had happened. I couldn't talk about him, I couldn't think about him, I didn't dream of him. I've heard that when you start to dream of what you have lost, it means the hurt is healing.

When I learned to speak of Rei, I showed Momo his photograph. She never asked until I was able to talk about him. She comprehended. Her body knew. Knew it was useless to ask.

I told her only that he had vanished. I couldn't think straight. We fell in love and married, we lived happily together, a child was born. We lived happily with our child, right up until the time he vanished. It would have been fair to tell her all this, but I didn't.

Momo was eight when I told her, and she didn't say much of anything. Only later, when she entered junior high, did she tell me how she had felt.

Back then, I didn't really understand your explanation. Daddy left, you told me, right, and so I just thought it was a terrible thing to do. He wasn't there anymore, so it didn't matter, he could be terrible or not, it didn't matter. This is what she told me in junior high.

"Did you and Daddy love each other?" she asked. Perched on the boulder.

"Yes."

Even as I replied, I was jolted by the words: *love each other.* The stray strand of hair drifted up lightly on the wind. Her forehead is bare. Her eyebrows are like Rei's. The easy, gentle curve.

"I wonder what it would be like if he were here."

"There's no telling."

"You had a father, you must know."

"He was a totally different person from your father."

"So it's different, then, with different fathers?" Momo said, blinking her eyes. "It's chilly, huh? Do you want to head back?"

The handkerchiefs we had spread to sit on were damp, the colors vivid. For the first time in ages, Momo and I held hands. Such a sturdy hand. It's as big as mine. We don't talk much about Dad, do we? I said as we headed back. I never dream of Rei, even now.

ON THE WAY back, something followed. It was the woman.

She stayed for dinner, too. Snatching food, eating. Momo's food, mine. She appeared to be fond of shrimp, kept plucking them from a plate of seafood in tomato sauce. She stole the same pieces repeatedly, as long as they stayed on the plate. The food itself remained even after she had taken and eaten it, so she could steal it again and again.

"You must be famished," I said. The woman nodded.

"I'm just getting started," Momo replied, too.

I wasn't talking to you. I spoke the words inside, not aloud. What a good child, responding so politely—a good, obliging child. I gave Momo a warm, cheerful smile. The woman grimaced. Like a burst of electric current, a flash of numbness.

Eventually I realized that I was angry. The woman fled. I will not allow anything to come between Momo and me. This, I realized, was the thought I had been thinking.

Out on the shore, I had become closer. Closer with Momo. I want to be close with Momo. That's what I am after. But not Momo. She becomes distant. Draws slightly closer. And then withdraws again. So smoothly, aware or unaware, she repeats the cycle.

I will not allow it. I hadn't felt like this since Momo was a baby. In those days, it wasn't even a matter of allowing, forbidding, nothing could intrude between Momo and me. Because we were close in those days—every day, all day. It was far from fun. It was exhausting. I held myself still, like a crouching animal, passing time. Nursing, cooking, sweeping, dusting, drying, folding, my body was ceaselessly busy, forever active, but my gaze was never turned outward. Frozen, crouching, my gaze still.

"Something went by just now," Momo said.

"What?"

"An airplane, maybe."

It wasn't the woman. Momo was looking at the sky. Our round table was by the window, nothing outside but the sweep of ocean and sky. From time to time, the waiter came to check how much food was left on our plates.

That was delicious, Momo said, glancing up at the waiter when he came to clear the table. Thank you, I'm happy to hear that, the waiter replied, beaming. The woman came back over.

Do you know Rei? I asked the woman.

Momo was asleep. In the other bed, curled up, a tight, delicate bump. I couldn't hear her breathing. Only a sort of sigh that escaped when she turned.

Rei? The woman asked.

My husband.

The woman had followed as I drew the bath, and as we watched television after our baths, and as we went out onto the terrace to breathe the still night air. She had something to say.

I know him, I think, said the woman. She was there erratically, growing faint one second, then suddenly more intense. She possessed no clear form to begin with, of course. Only I was aware she was following. I was the one who felt her eating shrimp, grimacing at me, and if you were to tell me there was no woman there at all, that would be the end of it.

Is Rei alive?

I don't know.

Where did you meet him?

I forget.

The woman's replies were unsatisfactory. Since we had come to Manazuru, she had grown more intense, it was true, but there was no sense in probing further. I tried to sleep, but the woman distracted me. I wanted her to leave.

Go away already.

Where to?

Where you usually are.

But I don't know where that is.

The woman was at a loss. Very well, but there was nothing I could do to help her. I kicked off the covers. The air conditioning was set low, I couldn't be hot, and yet my body was burning. It was all so strange. I had never talked to one before.

Everything is such a mess. I thought. Then, all of a sudden, she was gone.

The things that come and follow me don't interest me. I don't care. Whether or not they are there makes no difference to me. I feel like a scale with no weights resting in its pan. The weights have been removed, the scale rocks. You can't tell from the rocking which side was heavier. All you can say for sure is that gradually the rocking will subside. I feel lonely.

"COME ON, MA, perk up," Momo said.

The morning light was strong. We were having a Japanese breakfast in the same restaurant where we had eaten the previous evening. The hotel had more guests than I had thought. Only two tables were occupied then; now there was someone in almost every seat.

Dried mackerel, miso soup with daikon, and slices of deep-fried tofu. Boiled spinach drizzled with soy sauce, boiled tofu. I'm not *not* perky, I said, and Momo laughed. Then why are you eating so little?

I hadn't touched the mackerel or tofu. Momo seemed to want them, so I let her have both. Growing children, you know, we've got appetites, Momo said, refilling her rice bowl.

The brightness of late afternoon is not the same as the brightness of morning. Start with a clean slate, I murmured. What? Momo asked.

That's how morning feels, don't you think?

I told you you weren't very perky. Were you thinking about Dad and stuff?

Momo strips the mackerel, leaving the spine and the head, picking out the eyeballs, and cleans her plate. Rei liked fish, too. I have no desire to remember Rei, not now, not in the morning. Think of Seiji instead. That's hardly fair to Seiji. To think of him solely to avoid thinking of another.

"How about you, Momo? Is there a boy you like?" I asked.

"Yes and no."

"What's he like?"

"Ordinary."

I had readied myself for sullenness, but she replied jubilantly. I felt slightly happy, too.

"What do you like about him?"

"He's nice."

I laughed. Momo sulked. I had laughed too much. I was amused by the words *he's nice*. Momo is so adorable, I stroked her cheek. All at once she paled. She shook her head violently, rejecting the hand I touched her with. She wanted to be distant. From me.

These things are hard, I thought. I got to my feet. Walking back to the room, a long, long way behind me, Momo followed. And between her and me, the woman.

"How was Manazuru?" Mother asked.

"We went to Atami, too," Momo told her. After checking out of the hotel, we changed our minds about going home and took a trip to Atami. I thought that with Momo, the tumult of my heart would be soothed by that town's crowded, commercialized, flat scenery.

We stopped for cake. We roamed aimlessly, left behind the strip of souvenir shops that stretched from the station, traced the course of the river as it ran toward the sea, and stumbled across a small pastry shop. There was a shooting gallery on the other side of the river. The shooting gallery was closed up, silent—perhaps it had gone out of business. The pastry shop was newly built, though a sign said it had been around for decades.

The chocolate cake was good, Momo said. We had milk, too. Warm milk. In the shop, I noticed that the back of Momo's neck smelled. It smelled sweet. Her growing up repulses me. It is not *her* growing that disgusts me, but the growing itself. She casts off unneeded things. So many things. She can't help herself. And so I pity her. Her youth, her ignorance.

What is it that repulses me? The burgeoning? Of her body, her emotions. It occurs to me that I am repulsed, as well, by the sight of pregnant women. I myself, pregnant with Momo, was more than I could bear.

We took many pictures in Atami. The woman didn't come. She had disappeared, suddenly, as the train passed through Yugawara. The sense of Rei's presence, too, had faded. When we had the photos developed, Momo was smiling in every one.

"My smile looks kind of fake," Momo said, pointing to her face.

"It's a nice smile, you look happy."

"You look exactly like your mother when you smile," Mother said.

On the train back, I had gazed out the window at the town of Manazuru. Clouds hung over it. In Atami, the sky was clear. Something unquiet shrouded Manazuru. The people who live there don't know it. Only the passersby can tell.

Next time, all three of us should go somewhere, I said, glancing at Mother. Her expression said: I pity you. In Mother's eyes, I am young, and ignorant.

I AM AFLUTTER when I go to meet Seiji. We have been together for ages now, yet every time I see him, my heart dances.

"I went on a trip with my daughter," I tell him.

"Was the weather nice?"

"Half and half."

I talk to him, excitedly, of many things that make no sense. I talk as we walk. I am unable to make necessary adjustments, to talk of one thing but not another. I am like a coarse sieve—no matter what you put in, it drops through.

"I get sleepy when I'm with you," Seiji once told me.

"You mean I bore you?" I asked, nervous.

"No, not that, it's more a peaceful sleepiness," he replied, smiling.

Sometimes I feel my age. Ten years have gone by since I met Seiji. The same accumulation of time ages us differently. He grows older at his pace and I grow older at mine, and our times keep time separately. We do not flow in the same way.

"But it holds together."

"What does?" Seiji asked.

"The whole thing."

"You think?"

Seiji didn't press me. The whole thing. I wasn't sure what I meant. But it was true.

"I tried to call you," Seiji said quietly.

"When?"

"While you were in Manazuru."

You did? I asked, startled. I hadn't seen any call on my cell phone. I remembered how deep the night had been in the hotel in Manazuru. The ocean rushing in, but seeming also to open out. The ocean went on and on, distant. How would it have felt to hear Seiji's voice in Manazuru?

I want you, I said. All right, then, we'll make love today, Seiji answered. Our bodies, as we stood there, side by side, radiated heat.

I SHY AWAY, just a little, until we start. Emotionally, physically, both.

I hesitate to begin. Ever so slightly, I demur.

"Come here," Seiji says, and I slide over. Once we touch, I am willing.

Seiji's palms are soft. The tips of my fingers are always stiff at first, so I feel his softness more. Soon my fingers limber. A smooth tide rocks the stagnant pool of blood deep in the core of my body, and the liquid flows to my extremities.

That's nice, I whisper. With Seiji, I use words. With Rei, I never could.

When we embrace, I feel as though I am only the outline of my body. My body's outline traces Seiji's. Two outlines almost fusing, but without dissolving, only what is contained within is swept together, leveled, blown again into a heap.

Afterward, even more than during our lovemaking, my body loosens, and for a time I am unable to move. For a time, in this case, meaning five minutes or so.

As I lie there, I hear a sound like the hissing of the tide.

"What's that sound?" I ask Seiji, and he cocks his head.

"You mean that car driving away?" he replied.

"The sound of a car driving, not close, but away?"

"If the car is approaching," Seiji says, pressing his cheek to the sheet, "it sounds sharper."

It strikes me that Seiji says things that are almost broken. Whether a car is coming or going, its velocity increases as it passes, there's no way to tell the difference. I am tempted to protest. I can't help wanting to say the words, to take what is almost broken, and break it.

"I'm hungry," I said in an intentionally husky voice. Seiji laughed. The almost brokenness dispersed.

"I feel like having something warm," I said, sitting up. I was capable of movement. I drew my finger lightly down his back. He kept his back straight, but his shoulders trembled.

Do you feel it? I asked, and he replied, It tickles.

I stretched, then touched Seiji again. The place where I touched him shrank from me. The roaring of the tide grew louder.

WE COUPLE, AND then we eat, we part, we go home.

I am light on the way back. Light and cool, no matter the time. In the day, at night, in the winter, in the summer. Cool and light.

While I was waiting in front of the station for the light to change, before the red had turned, a man wearing a hat stepped into the street without looking, and didn't stop.

"Watch out!" I cried. A white car was heading this way, speeding up. The man neither quickened nor slowed his pace, he went on walking, unperturbed.

My heart was pounding. Normally I don't think of my heart, but when I'm startled, it pounds. I understand that it is beating. The man ducked immediately into a side street. The light turned green, and the crowd welled into the crosswalk. A woman was walking next to me. She was my height, with short hair, stocky, she took her time crossing the street.

The beating of my heart attuned me to my body. To the movement of my feet. The steps of the woman beside me were synchronized with mine. Everyone in the crosswalk was walking at the same pace. I felt sick to my stomach.

I was feeling light, cool, but now I am being drawn into something odd.

To staunch this feeling, I think of Seiji. You don't have to feel when you are thinking. The callus, a small bulge on the middle finger of his right hand, above the joint, from his pencil. No one uses pencils anymore, I said to him once. Seiji shook his head. I do. Most of the time, I use a pencil, not a pen.

Seiji and I both work with writing. I am a writer. Writers write for Seiji. In the beginning, he and I worked together on a few projects. Each week, I would write a short essay. Seiji gives praise in a way unique to him. He praises without seeming to. The essays were published as a book, and more work came. I could take care of Momo, now. And myself.

I was still thinking when I reached our house. I stood still for a time in the glow of the streetlight. There had been such a crowd in front of the station, but somewhere along the way I had been left alone. Where does a crowd like that go off to?

When we left the hotel, Seiji said he was going back to the office. He flagged down a cab. As he climbed in, his back belonged to no one I knew. Sometimes these moments come.

And yet Rei never looked unfamiliar to me. Even now I can draw his face and body, everything, leaving nothing out. The street light shines so dimly. I stepped away from the light and quietly pushed open the gate to our house.

STILL THE SAME number of pills.

Mother takes medicine for her high blood pressure each morning and night. Her blood pressure tends to climb in the winter so she takes twice as many pills then; eventually, when spring arrives, she goes back to the usual dosage.

This year, even this late, I still need the same number.

She sounds disheartened. Maybe it's the doctor, I have a new doctor, now, a younger one. He does everything by the numbers. Old doctors understand, make adjustments.

She is stretching her arms as she speaks. Her tone is disheartened, but I can see her body is opening to the spring. When she stretches, strength flows into the tips of her fingers.

You'll go back to the usual number soon enough, I say, and Mother nods. Oh. I saw some tadpoles, she says, out of nowhere.

Where? I ask. Hmm. She giggles. Momo and I walked to the pond over at the university. On Sunday. While you were off at the movies by yourself.

That was work, you know, I muttered, as if making an excuse, and again Mother chuckled. Nothing wrong with a movie, you're welcome to go to as many as you like.

I always stiffened when I talked with Mother about Rei. She never tried to look at him, at Rei, the man I was married to, except through a sort of fish-eye lens. I don't mean she saw him from a prejudiced perspective. She was unwilling to regard him as a man with a form. She preferred to peer through her lens at his distorted, bulging toes, or at his ballooning head. Nothing else. She didn't dislike him enough to look away. She didn't hate him enough to stare. She chose to keep him indistinct.

Talking to Mother about my work is a little, a very little, like talking about Rei. But work is only work. It is like the salt and water you set out as an offering on the household shrine. The things are there, but since their meaning transcends you, you cease to notice them. Rei possessed a body. This, for Mother, was hard to bear.

Tadpoles, already? It seems too cold, I said. Mother cocked her head. Oops, did I say tadpoles? I meant eggs. They were still eggs. Those lines, like gelatin, covered with black dots. Can you believe that Momo says she's never seen them before?

The university is a twenty-minute walk away. The pond abuts the tennis courts. Rei and I went there a few times, I remembered, before we were married, on walks. The pond was small. Enclosed in untended growth, so that from the water's edge we couldn't see the tennis courts. We could only hear the thwack of the balls, so close it was eerie. Rei used to kiss me there, under the cover of the growth. Whispering my name, *Kei*, he kissed me.

No matter the season, the water always buzzed.

WHEN THE DAYS grew warmer, Momo went and caught some tadpoles. She scooped ten into a wide-mouthed glass jar.

"Water," Momo sighed, holding the jar up to the sunlight. "All this stuff floating in water."

Aligning my face with Momo's, I joined her, peering up into the jar. Miniscule bits of something like seaweed. Dashes of gray, like filaments of thread. Bits of soil. At first glance the water seemed transparent, but it was true, all manner of things hung suspended in it. Among them, the tadpoles, several of them, shuddered as they swam.

"Is it pond water?" I asked. Momo nodded. Funny, it looked so clean when I put it in the jar.

"Oh, it's nothing, that's what pond water looks like," I said. Again Momo eyed the jar.

The next morning one tadpole had died and was floating on the water's surface, but the rest were swimming around energetically. See how thin their tails are. Momo smiles. I love how thin they are, it's so cute.

After Momo left for school, a hush fell over the house. Mother was still asleep. I washed the dishes, set them into the drying rack. Water dripped. Catching the morning light, the drops were small and strong and intense. Are there things, all manner of tiny things, floating in these droplets, too? I wondered. Invisible swarms.

Sometimes, rarely, they come in swarms. Not, as a rule, when I am in a crowd, but in places devoid of people. Twenty, thirty at a time. It only lasts a moment, and then they are gone.

I opened my laptop on the kitchen table. Until recently, Momo called this silver machine "little Ginzō." *Gin* for silver. So it's a boy? I asked. Because, she told me, there aren't any boys in this house. She christened the computer soon after she started junior high. How sullen she has become in these three years.

A tub of margarine, sitting diagonally across from my computer, had been left with the lid ajar, and I could see how the margarine had softened. Its whitish yellowness looks cool when it is hard; when it softens, I want to touch it. To put a finger there, depress its surface, then lick off what clings to my skin. But I don't.

I closed the lid and put the container in the refrigerator. The fridge began to hum.

SOON AFTER THEY sprouted hind legs, as their front legs started to bud, six tadpoles died. Momo cried. She wrapped the nearly tailless six in gauze and buried them in the garden.

You've never had a pet before, Momo, have you? Mother said, stroking her head. You had a dog once, Kei, remember? You even built a doghouse. You bought a kit, and painted the roof red, Mother said, and Momo looked up.

What kind of dog was it? Momo asked.

A mutt.

What was its name?

Jirō.

When did he . . .

Twenty years ago.

Was he cute?

Yes.

Three of the tadpoles in the glass jar were still swimming. Their tails were longer than those of the six that died. Perhaps they too would die when their tails disappeared. I wonder if it's what I'm feeding them, Momo said. I'll go ask at the pet shop at the station. Maybe we need a proper aquarium.

I have errands to run, I'll come with you, Mother said, and began getting her things together. I wouldn't want a dog, Momo was saying. They're so adorable, I'd be frightened, she was saying.

"Frightened?" Mother asked.

Mmm. Frightened it would leave.

Mother falls silent. I fall silent as well. Momo keeps her head down as she buttons her jacket. Lately, we don't go out of our way to talk about Rei's disappearance, but we no longer avoid the topic. Jirō was a very smart dog. He could tell when it was all right to bark and when it wasn't. His fur tended to clump, and he always looked out of sorts. Whenever you petted him, his tail would stick up, and he would be so happy.

The soil in the garden where Momo buried the tadpoles was moist and dark, mossy green. Each time she thrust the shovel in, the earth crumbled.

IT WAS A dark green blazer.

The last summer blazer Rei bought. We're not supposed to wear ties on Fridays anymore. What a hassle, he said, as we headed to the department store. Rei didn't like shopping for clothes. After we married, he made me shop for him. Don't you have a preference in ties, at least? I asked, but he shook his head. I don't care, as long as there are no panthers, or dragons.

And yet, this time, he suggested a white jacket. I think a darker color might be better, considering the slacks you have, I told him, and he nodded.

There was, however, a brief moment of vacillation. So it seemed to me later. At the time, I didn't notice any wavering of his.

At home, I clipped off the price tag, paired the jacket with the slacks hanging in the wardrobe, and said, Yes, this was definitely the better color. Rei said nothing. I thought he hadn't heard. He wore the jacket to work a few times. Then he went back to neckties. They say we're not supposed to wear them, but about half the people still do. I'm a formal type, anyway, he grumbled.

Summer had just passed when Rei disappeared. Not long before, checking the blazer's pockets before taking it to the cleaners, I found a slip of paper. In the breast pocket. With a number, an hour, it seemed, written on it.

21:00

The slip of paper was the size of a business card, and the tiny numerals were written in one corner. I crumpled it and threw it away.

For a month after it became clear that Rei had disappeared, I didn't pick up the blazer at the cleaners. When I found the receipt in my wallet, I forced myself to go get it. On the way, I recalled the 21:00. My heart pounded.

It was still pounding as I opened the door of the cleaners. The woman behind the counter was sweating profusely. I don't do well with air conditioning, she said. Shortly before summer, she would begin repeating this, justifying herself, as her customers complained. Long after summer ended, the woman continued to sweat. She smelled, faintly.

I left the plastic bag on the blazer and pushed it deep into the closet. Until the day I packed our things to move in with Mother, I never touched it.

I WONDER WHAT Rei was thinking when he wrote that number. 21:00.

Wondering leads nowhere. Little by little, as time passes, the hurt Rei left fades. I threw the blazer out a few years ago. Even so, there is no shortage of proof that he existed.

"Seiji." I spoke his name into the phone. Saying it over the phone brings him closer. More so than when he is here, with me. Because the ear concentrates the sound, perhaps.

"Yes?"

"Will we break up, eventually, you and me?"

"That's an unexpected question," Seiji said. "Do you want to break up?"

"No, I was just remembering."

Seiji knows that when I tell him I remember, I am not speaking about him, but about Rei. It's a terrible way to be. I think so myself. Of myself.

Seiji is so good. He never says anything that isn't good. So he scares me. Frightens me in a different way, not like Rei.

"If you were meeting someone at nine at night, where would you meet?" I asked.

"That's a hard one. By then most cafes are closed. A hotel lobby. Or a lounge. Maybe a bar would be best." He answers me seriously, carefully.

I can't even be certain that the number 21:00 marked the time of a meeting. I am simply playing, clinging to my dead-end wondering.

"I'm meeting someone at nine tonight myself," Seiji said on the other end.

Oh.

"An old classmate, younger than me, in a hotel bar."

"Well, take care," I said, and Seiji smiled. He didn't laugh aloud, he never does, but I could sense the outward movement of the air around his mouth.

Could Rei's disappearance have been avoided if I had told him to take care? Wondering, again, leads nowhere. I straighten my back, quiet my need to be comforted. I ask Seiji brusquely when we will see each other. I'm busy this month, I may not have time, I'm sorry, Seiji says.

That's okay, I understand. I don't protest. Seiji smiles again. You're quiet today.

When he said he couldn't see me, my chest ached. I didn't miss him, I ached.

THERE WAS MORE than the slip of paper.

I have Rei's diary, too. It sits next to the dictionaries, on the bookshelf. Once a month or so, I flip through its pages.

It is a diary of notes. "1 pack razor blades." "Torigen tonight." "Takamatsu." "Kawahara." "Section chief paid for dinner." "Momo's horse figurine." Such things, written, utterly flat. None of the words have any life, yet every time I read them I am wounded. The mere sight of the words, lined up on the pages, cuts into me.

I hadn't known Rei kept a diary. At first, when I found it, I pored carefully over it hoping it might contain a clue to his disappearance. Some murkiness—a woman, money. I searched for anything unclear.

I didn't find anything. I sat dazed for a time. Not because I had failed, but because I had been afforded a glimpse of Rei's life. The words, the cost of a bowl of chicken-and-egg-over-rice he'd had for lunch, a list of the back issues of a magazine, a note from work: "delivery five days early, negotiations tomorrow," refused absolutely to connect to the person who had been here with me until recently, to Rei.

I moved the diary behind other books for a time. So I wouldn't have to see it. Rei had never looked like a stranger to me, not for an instant, and yet suddenly, reading his diary, he was someone I didn't know. I couldn't recall his face. His smell. The feel of his skin. His voice.

It wasn't because he was gone. It was because, reading his diary, I was seeing the things around me, not with my own eyes, but with his. It was sickening to view things through another's eyes. Since then, to read his diary hurts. I ache. No. I refuse. Him, Rei. He is separate from me. A barrier stands between him and me.

Yet I always knew the barrier was there. I knew it, but it comes as a shock, having to confront it. I am emotionally seared, as when a flame licks forward, and you leap back.

After a time, I brought the diary back out to the front. To the shelf reserved for the books I use. *Stupid Rei.* Sometimes I say this. In a faint way, I say it, to see how it feels.

Once, as I said the words, Momo was gazing at me, fixedly, unseen. From behind.

She left right away as I remained motionless, the open diary in my hand. Antipathy. That's not the word, precisely, but I sensed a thick anger radiating. From behind.

I envied her anger. Try as I might to get angry, it slips away. There is nothing for me to seize onto, and so I reach out, and my hand passes right through all that I have.

THE TREES BLOSSOM, and the air is scented.

I can't see Seiji, and now that Momo has started high school, she is busy. I walked alone to the university. It feels good when the sky is so clear. I went to the pond by the tennis courts and sat on the grass. The last three of Momo's tadpoles grew into frogs. Not long ago, Momo and I came to this pond and released them. The small green frogs sat motionless for some time on the grass, then leaped, vanishing into the underbrush, hopping in low, minute arcs.

On days when the sky is clear, the things that come and follow me shine. The pond water buzzes. I open a can of tea that I bought on the way and drink. I'm thirsty. I realize as I drink that I have been thirsty. It is a man who comes. I may have known him once. The thought crosses my mind as I gulp my tea.

I take Rei's diary from my bag. Open it, tear out a random page. Once a year, or so, I do this. Eventually, I hope, I will tear all the pages out. I start making an airplane. I will send it flying onto the surface of the pond, let it sink.

My fingers, folding the sheet of paper, brush over Rei's handwriting. A bit below the thick black words—TWENTY ¥62 STAMPS. SAITŌ CO. DONE—written with a fountain pen, is the word MANAZURU. It jolts me. I undo the folds and look closer. On a date one month before his disappearance, in a ballpoint pen's thin strokes, he had written *Manazuru*.

I fold the sheet of paper into a square and stick it back between the diary's pages. *Ma. Na. Zu. Ru.* I whisper the syllables. I hadn't noticed. Or had I forgotten? *Ma. Na. Zu. Ru.* Once again, I say the word. The surface of the pond sparkles. The thing following me, too, is sparkling. The wind rises. The space around me is filled by the rustling of leaves. I can't see for all the light.

three

I SAW A CAMELLIA blossom fall.
I had seen crimson petals scattered on the ground, like water drops, and I had seen those bulky blossoms capsized whole in dirt, but I had never actually seen one fall.

"Look," I said, and Rei, walking beside me, quickly glanced over.

"It dropped, huh?" Rei said, then bent and scooped the blossom up.

It was no different from when it had still been on the tree.

Without a word, Rei clenched it in his fist. Large petals fluttered down. Slipping through his bent fingers, a few petals at a time. Finally only the yellow core remained. Rei crushed it, too.

"There's pollen in my hand," he said, opening his fist. The undone weave of stamens, pistil, calyx, and the fine petals at the center, fell more slowly than the larger petals.

"Poor thing," I said.

Rei turned to look at me. Why?

To destroy it like that.

It would have rotted anyway, eventually.

We had been a couple for some time by then. I thought him heartless. *Rei*. I spoke his name, to see how it would feel. Usually it didn't come easily; this time it came right out.

Kei, he replied. One of the fingers that had toyed with the camellia entered my mouth. For a moment the strong sweet scent of the flower's core wafted up, and then, without realizing what had happened, I was sucking. Sucking on his finger.

Occasionally, when I started nursing Momo, I recalled that sensation. Sucking Rei's finger. I sucked like a baby. At the time I didn't notice, I only realized it when I started nursing Momo. Utterly, sweetly, painfully engrossed, sucking, heedless, the finger he held out.

REI WAS LIKE the retreating tide.

Try to stand your ground, still it draws your body in.

Rei drew me in. He was a master of the surprise attack. You think he is flat, uninteresting, you cease to pay attention, and he sweeps you off your feet. Less than two months after we started dating, I couldn't get him out of my mind.

Our first night together, we stayed in Hakone. We met at dusk, in Shinjuku. We didn't know where we would go, but we had decided that we would spend the night.

"Let's take the Romance Train," Rei announced, and purchased our tickets. I still remember the sound of my ticket being punched when I presented it at the gate.

We switched at Yumoto to the Tozan Line and got off at one of the stations along the way. The road shot straight up the mountain; walking, we came to an inn.

"We'll stay here, then?" Rei said.

As he slid open the frosted-glass door, an old pendulum clock, hanging to one side, came into view. A woman sat behind the counter. She walked out, a pair of slippers in each hand, and aligned the slippers on the floor.

"How much a night?" Rei asked.

Seven thousand yen each, dinner and breakfast included, she replied. All right, we'll stay, Rei told her without missing a beat, and the woman promptly led us to our room.

Rei tore the paper wrapper from a sweet on the table and popped it whole into his mouth. Shall I make some tea? I asked. It's okay, I can do it, he answered.

I went to soak in the bath. When I returned, Rei was stretched out on the floor. The top of his light cotton kimono hung open; he had propped himself up, a tea cup at his elbow.

Want some? he asked, and when I asked, Tea? he said, No, whiskey, it was in the fridge.

Gotta have booze, right? It would have been awkward without it, just the two of us at an inn like that, Rei explained later. We finished dinner and set out on a walk in the kimonos the inn provided. The mountain road was dark. The clatter of our wooden clogs on the asphalt reverberated stiffly through the air. I could smell the alcohol on Rei's breath.

I had gotten rooms with men before, but they always wore themselves out trying to make our time together festive, from start to finish. With Rei, the air was clear. Every unnecessary sound, the heat of our bodies, siphoned away, vanished. We did not exhilarate, we were not warmed.

And so, all the more, he drew me in.

IT WAS EARLY summer when we were in Hakone.

As dawn broke on the mountain, before it was fully light, we briefly loved. It was deeper than when we had embraced in the evening. As we were paying at the desk, I suddenly pictured the daybreak tangle of our bodies, and became wet. The rainy season was unusually long that year. We sauntered through a light rain, sharing an umbrella. Nesting dolls were arrayed on a glass shelf in a souvenir shop. They looked just like Russian matryoshka dolls, seven sizes, big to small, each one progressively smaller, lined up in a row.

How adorable, I said, and Rei asked, You want them? When I hesitated, offering no reply, he picked them up and took them wordlessly to the salesperson. He paid, then stuffed the purchase into my bag. I never bought a woman anything, he told me on the Romance Train on the way back. It was a surprise. Your first present, and you get these? Smiling broadly, I popped the dolls open at the torso, unnesting them, and lined them up on the windowsill. The smallest, cradled at the center, was about as big around as a one-yen coin.

One after the other, Rei tapped each empty, hollow doll with his fingernail. They didn't make much of a sound. A half-hearted *thwack*.

I never went anywhere with a woman without wanting to skip out on her, either, Rei said when we got off the train, merging with the Shinjuku crowds.

Skip out? Laughing, I lifted my face and peered at him. There was almost a smile on his face, but it wasn't a smile, his expression was sour.

Reluctant to part, we found a backstreet bar, a *yakitori* place, and went in, even though it was early, even though the sun had yet to set. We ordered two large mugs of draft beer, and as the sun finally began to sink, we relaxed. I didn't go home that night, I stayed for the first time at Rei's apartment. Before the night descended, early in the evening, already we were deep within it. By then, our bodies knew each other. Still embracing, we fell, almost fainting, asleep.

"MY, DOES THE gutter smell," Mother says.

"I don't think there are any gutters left around here," I tell her. When I played ball as a child, the ball was always rolling into the gutters that ran along both sides of the street. I would dry the surface, which glistened from the trickle of drainage, by wiping it on the street. Then, years later, the gutters were filled in, and the smell dispersed.

"It smells like stagnant water, though."

Maybe when the wind is just right it blows here all the way from the river, I say. Mother closes her eyes. She breathes deeply. But the river is in the next district. Kind of far, isn't it?

Come to think of it, Mother goes on, these past few years, it has hardly rained at all during the rainy season. "An empty rainy season." We get a good deal more precipitation earlier on, in the "rapeseed rainy spell," as it's called, spring showers, than during the true rainy season.

I, too, inhale. From time to time the scent of water drifts over, strong. It smells this way when a hot, clear day follows upon a period of rain. Empty rainy season, rapeseed rainy spell. I think the words. When I was young, in early summer, my body seemed to be bleeding outward, past its edges; now, year by year, that feeling fades. I sensed myself blurring when I started to stay over at Rei's apartment, too. Not only at the end of the rainy season, at other times as well. Hard as I struggled to contain it, something leaked. After I was married, after I gave birth to Momo, even then my body blurred. It was more than the fluids secreted by the dark, soft place; I seemed to feel something bleeding out from behind my eyes. The scent of early summer made me giddy, for just a moment. It still does.

I am rereading the diary, carefully. I have slipped the folded page that says *Manazuru* back into the diary, after the final page. There is nothing new in this diary. Everything written here remains the same as the last time I checked. I can only read from it what I have already read.

I THINK I'M pregnant, I told Rei. I couldn't remember when.

But it was there, recorded in his diary.

"A baby. Due next April. Kei looked like a fish when she told me." One of the rare entries with a personal touch. What's that supposed to mean, I looked like a fish? I was too distraught when I first read the diary, in the aftermath of Rei's disappearance, to respond to much of anything, and yet I laughed at that.

The morning sickness was awful. Less than two weeks after the fertilized egg attached itself to the wall of my uterus, I felt gray, excruciatingly. It would take more time to determine whether or not I was actually pregnant. I could tell, though, that a foreign body was in me. "A foreign body" sounds too charged, it was less than that, just a little thing that came in.

It astonished me that something smaller than the tip of my pinky could induce such nausea. It was this sickness that made me look like a fish.

There was only one other personal entry.

"A place I should never have come to."

The date is about a year before his disappearance. A place I should never have come to. Where was my husband when he felt this way? Then, under the same date:

"Agreement. Scrap."

I don't know if the meaning here is deep or shallow. I read it over and over and I still don't understand. The diary harbors, on the whole, no mysteries; only this one day's entry fills me with doubts.

My morning sickness continued for two months. Then, as soon as I entered the fifth month, it abruptly stopped. The embryo developing into a child inside me is not a foreign body now, I thought. I craved fatty foods; I had, surely, lost the fish look. By then I probably resembled some other sort of animal, some furry creature.

The whole time that the baby continued burgeoning inside me, my mind was shrouded in fog. I couldn't think straight. Only when I engaged in monotonous, repetitive activities would my body pick up the pace. I sewed any number of diapers, fixing bleached cotton cloth in a circle, turning it inside out, stitching it from the top. Nothing could persuade me to take such trouble now.

I don't remember what Rei was doing then, how he felt. I was enveloped in a cocoon, not unwilling to face the world, but unable to grasp, no matter how I tried, what went on there.

Not all pregnant women are this way. It could be that I am easily wounded, I mused, but I don't think so. On the contrary, it is hard to hurt me. Rei was different. He seemed unfazed, but he wasn't. He was closer, closer even than Seiji, to the breaking point. I can see that now.

THE PAIN, GIVING birth to Momo, was staggering.

Until then, I didn't know pain. I thought I did, but I was mistaken. It was not a momentary thing, a passing numbness, a faint spell; it was just pain. Unremitting, uniform.

And yet once I had borne her, I forgot. Completely forgot.

"Aren't you the cutest thing?" I said, unabashed, just one or two days after the delivery. I marveled at myself. After the agony I'd endured, hard like rage, coursing through my body, everywhere, finding no outlet, until I feared my body would be ripped to pieces, and yet I catch myself saying, lightly, unabashed, "There's my baby, yes, yes."

It's a travesty.

I thought. Lying in bed, doing the postpartum exercises. At the appointed moment, all at once, the new mothers began moving their hips and legs to the music blaring from the speakers.

It's worse than it seems. No, that isn't quite right.

Time heals all wounds. Close, but not exactly.

Different paths to the same conclusion. That's even further off the mark.

In our shared hospital room, doing the exercises, four new mothers chatting back and forth about the travesty of it all. It was incredible, too, that at the moment we had given birth, we came to regard each other as mothers. In the delivery room, seconds before we released our babies, we had still referred to each other, in our thoughts, by name.

The other "mothers," too, seemed to have been struck, each in her own way, by the puzzle of how we had felt before the birth and how we felt afterward.

"It was nothing like I expected," we repeated.

It was not a whole new world. But we had come to a different place. As time passed, from moment to moment, that place evolved. Evolved, kept changing, and we shuddered, unsure how far we would have to go, and then we came back, back here. Only not all the way.

The difference of the place had nothing to do with living and dying. It was simply different. Set apart from everyday life. Yet more and more, the everyday seemed to be bleeding in. Penetrating to the center, the very center of the pain. During the birth, at the soles of our feet as we strained against the tabletop, exerting ourselves, there was the utterly ordinary.

It was unfathomable. I talked it over with the other "mothers." And I forgot all of that, as well, in no time. After we gave the baby an actual person's name, called it "Momo," I thought of nothing but raising her.

A place I should never have come to. As I bore my child, during that time, I felt the terror of having taken just a step into that space. How linked was that feeling, I wonder, to the words my husband penned in his diary?

That feeling, after the birth, of being unable to return all the way, hasn't completely faded. It is with me, I think, until death. The morning Momo was born, sparrows sang in the trees.

"So," I ASKED Seiji, "did you meet your classmate, at nine, and have a few?"

The hour 21:00 was on my mind. Since I started rereading the diary, I couldn't shake it.

"They serve tempura at this bar," he said, answering a question I hadn't asked.

"Tempura?"

"Whitebait."

That's right, even though whitebait are in season in early spring, and it's nearly summer, he said, and smiled. My classmate drank a lot. I just had a couple.

What do you think people think at nine at night? I asked.

Hmm. I know how it feels at three A.M., or four, at daybreak.

I glanced at Seiji's reply. Three or four?

At three, a bit hopeful. At four, a bit despairing.

That's a lovely way of putting it.

You're mocking me. Weren't you? Just now.

I wasn't, actually. But it was too lovely. Hope and despair aren't so easily distinguished.

"Kei." For the first time in a long time, Seiji spoke my name.

"Yes?" I responded, as gently as I could.

"Don't make me think of things that aren't here."

I looked again at Seiji, taken aback. His face was pale. What's wrong? I stared.

"I'm jealous," he said.

Jealous. I gulped, just a little. Such an odd word. Hearing it from his mouth. Seiji is never supposed to say that, and yet he just has.

"But, he's not, you know, around anymore," I murmur.

Seiji clammed up. He has something he wants to tell me, I thought. But he couldn't say it. He seemed incapable of finding the words.

I leaned against him. For Seiji, married and with three kids, to be jealous of me, who had only Momo. It made no sense. Or are such things irrelevant? Having, missing.

"I get jealous because he's not around," Seiji said.

"I get jealous because he's not around, yet he follows you," he corrected himself.

He follows you.

I started at those words.

"You know about them, following me?" I asked.

"Following you," Seiji repeated vaguely. I saw that he had only chanced upon those words, he didn't know. I don't want Seiji to know, I thought.

Suddenly one came. It was extremely dense. Not human, something furry. A thing like me, when I entered my fifth month, after the morning sickness stopped.

I smelled water. I shook my head hard, and the thing went. Seiji said no more.

SHORTLY BEFORE HE disappeared, Rei scolded Momo.

Not in the reflexive way one reproves a three-year-old whose language is unformed, to keep her from doing something dangerous. He didn't scold, he remonstrated.

Momo had drawn on his papers. In crayons: red, yellow, pink.

Momo. Come here. I heard him calling from the entryway before he left for work. I was washing the dishes, and couldn't hear him well. I thought he was calling for me, I bustled out, wiping my hands on my apron, and found Momo sitting very small on the floor, her feet tucked under her. Rei sat with his feet tucked beneath him, too, not far from the door, looking constricted. His suit pants were wrinkled.

Holding the colored-on pages out to Momo, Rei explained why what she had done was bad. What is he thinking, explaining something like that to a three-year-old, I thought. But Momo sat still, listening. She was not an extraordinarily active child, but she was a child, and it must have been hard for her to sit without moving in such an uncomfortable position. Yet she didn't move.

Slumped over, she apologized. I'm sawwy, Daddy. Some children can pronounce their "r"s right away; some take forever to learn. Momo took forever. Momo won't cwayon anymow, she said, looking at his eyes. Rei nodded. You won't do it again, right?

They sat there for a time. When Rei rose, Momo began to weep.

Because she was frustrated by the scolding she had received, perhaps. Or because she had been released from the adult tension she had endured, the unfamiliar position, the apology. Or simply because her body needed to release that liquid. Rei stroked the top of Momo's head. There's a good girl, he said, gently stroking her.

I felt kind of like a father, he said that evening. You've been a father for years, I responded. He shook his head. It doesn't feel that way. It's not that easy.

On TV, the anchorman was reporting the results of the day's sumo matches, the September tournament. I never gave much thought to the word "family" back then. You don't think about the things you have. Only when they are gone do you begin.

In those days, too, things came and followed me. But they were very faint. So faint I could barely tell whether or not they were there. It is different now. It is perfectly clear, when they come, faint or thick, that they are there.

The *yokozuna* won today, the anchorman says, and the final match is broadcast. The crowd cheers. Rei glances at the screen.

I reached out, feeling myself blur, and placed my hand on Rei's neck as he stared at the TV. I touched him slowly, and he smiled. It was a deep, tender smile. Is this really how he smiles? I thought, taken aback. The blurring spread, wider and wider.

Not long after, Rei was gone.

"They were missing. I found them," Momo said.

"You lost something?" I asked, and Momo spread her palm, held it out.

"Look, these," she replied.

A few small objects, wrapped in silver foil, rolled in her hand.

"Chocolates?"

Yes, she nodded. A present. Valentine's day, she added.

"You got these?"

All the girls give them out. Not to boys, to their girlfriends.

You want one? Momo offered me a ball of silver foil. I picked at the tightly mashed edge of the foil, then peeled it away. A brown sphere appeared. I put it in my mouth. After sucking for a moment, I bit down, and a gooey liquid flowed out.

"They were all the way in the back of my desk." Peeling off the foil, Momo pops one after another into her mouth. There is a pimple on her cheek. Her pimples are small ripples of skin, here in the morning, gone by the evening. Her skin was always so smooth, but recently it has acquired a dimmer luster. Her skin was soft, clinging, the skin of a baby, but now it has begun to project, from inside, a hardness.

Presents are interesting, Momo says, mashing her jaw up and down as she chews her chocolates. I think I prefer getting presents I've been anticipating, rather than just being given one all of a sudden, out of the blue.

Startling to hear her make a comment so adult, like a grown woman.

"Is there something you want?" I ask. Just to see.

"I think so."

"What?"

She started to say something, then stopped. It isn't that she doesn't want to say it, I think, it's that she can't think how. Her mouth hangs slightly open as she wavers, and I can see, on the back of her tongue, a pale smudge of chocolate brown. Let me know when you figure out how to say it, okay? I say, and leave the room.

When, I wonder, did I stop blurring around the edges? I don't blur with Seiji. My shape is always the same, contained.

THE FIRST TIME I spent the night with Seiji, we stayed in an inn on the beach in Izu. I used work as an excuse, added an extra day to my trip, met up with him at the station.

We found the van to take us to the inn. The driver was not there, the doors were open. Seiji and I climbed in. Soon three older women boarded and filled the middle row of seats; then a couple in their twenties got in. Finally the driver came. I realized he was the same old man, wearing a sash, who had been angling for customers by the station.

The inn was large enough to accommodate tour groups. Awfully jolly, this place, isn't it, I remarked, and Seiji smiled. You would have preferred someplace less well lit, free from prying eyes?

We went off separately to the large, open baths, men's and women's, then, since there was still time before dinner, played ping-pong. The ping-pong room was carpeted, so we kicked off our slippers and played barefoot. We played hard. Beginning to sweat, we rolled our sleeves up to our shoulders.

"I feel like I'm on a field trip," I said, fanning my face with the paddle. Seiji seized this opening to smash the ball back. Chagrined, I put as much spin on the ball as I could the next time I served.

By the time we finished dinner, we were sleepy. We had already been to soak a second time in the baths after our ping-pong match. As we watched television in our room, it struck me that my travels with Rei had felt much more secretive. It was apparent to me that Seiji belonged to a family. Since Rei's disappearance, I had forgotten what family meant. What it meant to be a family, or to be in a family.

I switched off the television. Seiji and I lay face up on our futons, side by side, gazing at the ceiling. Come here, Seiji said. Just like always. I scooted over, we coupled, we parted, again we gazed at the ceiling. If I had married Seiji, it would have gone on like this, I thought, always. Not just the way we interacted, but some bond between us that took longer to form. It would have stayed, I thought, exactly as it was.

Longer. Prior to Mother. After Momo. Something that continues, unbroken.

It isn't only memory, neither is it anything as precisely structured as a gene. All one can say, in the end, is that it continues.

I fell asleep right away. I didn't wake, not once, until morning.

WOULD YOU LIKE to go somewhere, for a change? Seiji asked.

Where? I asked back.

You went to Manazuru with Momo, right?

I haven't told Seiji of my first trip, alone, to Manazuru. That might be nice, I say, reserving an ambiguity. After ten years, surprise, I've spent more time with Seiji than with my husband.

I'd like to go to the end of the earth, I say quietly.

Which end in particular? South? North? West? East?

So like him to take me literally. Not the North Pole. Too cold. Not the South Pole, either.

As I replied, equally literally, I began to grow sleepy. It is so ordinary with Seiji. It is hard to be ordinary. Extraordinary things abound. But the extraordinary usually can't be sustained. Sooner or later, it breaks. Beyond the break it is easy. Keeping it ordinary is hardest of all.

What are you thinking? Seiji asks.

Nothing interesting, I say.

I think more, now, of Seiji. In the beginning, the ordinariness of it never even struck me. Did Rei ever think of me? I feel my expression cloud.

"There you go again," Seiji says, "with what isn't here."

"How could you tell?" I ask, taken aback.

"Because, you're like that lately."

Is he jealous again? If so, it's frequent. Before, the word *jealousy* didn't figure.

Overcome by tenderness for Seiji, I hug him. You hug like my mother, Seiji says.

I'm not your mother. I'm me. It's me, you know? I say, hugging him stronger. A woman comes. The woman who followed me when I went to Manazuru, both times. Who is bidding me, constantly, to go to Manazuru.

Seiji, don't go, I say, hugging him so tight it hurts. His arms hang, and he is still.

IT GOT HOT early, so we put away our winter clothes twice this year.

Once, soon after the tadpoles Momo scooped up sprouted limbs. Again, at the end of June, midway through the rainy season.

"You don't smell the naphthalene anymore," Mother says. Before Momo was born, we used to cut small incisions in the corners of cellophane packets, each of which contained two balls of naphthalene, and tossed several into each drawer in the chest.

"These new ones don't smell like anything, huh." Mother presses her nose to the package and frowns. There's nothing to miss in these.

Putting away clothes at the end of June is a bother. Push the heavy jackets to the back of the closet, bring the lightest ones to the front. Put all the end-of-winter outfits that haven't yet gone to the cleaners in a single bag to be taken there later.

Mother is trying on a sleeveless blouse she bought last year, massaging her slender arms. "As wrinkly as crepe paper," she whispers. "Look at this, when I push the skin up, just look." She told me to touch it, and I put a fingertip against her upper arm, simply to oblige her. Her skin was half desiccated. It gathered in neat folds, like windswept sand.

"It's only half dried up, so it doesn't wrinkle unless you press it."

Enthralled, Mother squeezed innumerable crepe wrinkles into her skin, above her elbow and below it. This is what happens when you grow old, I guess. A few more years and I'll be all dried up, I'll have wrinkles all the time, without making them, she says, impressed.

I don't often do household chores with Mother. When we move around in the same area, the space grows hot. When we work separately, we stay cool.

"It's fun rearranging our wardrobes together," Mother smiles. When we get ready for winter, let's have Momo help, I murmur in response.

Handling so many different fabrics, heavy clothes, light clothes, makes my palms feel silky. I rise quietly, take the folded material from here to there. Bend down, lay it in a box. In the same motion, I take the next piece from the box. Fabric brushing against fabric, making the merest sound. Two women, one getting on in years, one starting to get on in years, pacing among the fabrics. With the tips of my fingers, I tear off the paper tag the cleaners stapled to the label last year. Replace the paper that lines the drawer, fold the old paper, throw it out. Straighten the new paper in the drawer, pile in the different materials, layer upon layer.

Each time we change winter clothes for summer, summer clothes for winter, I find items I no longer need. Sometimes I pack away clothes I know I will never wear. Sometimes I unpack something, only to realize that its time has come. I cut some up to use as rags. Some I pass on as hand-me-downs to younger relatives. Some I throw away. I remove the buttons from heavier articles before I get rid of them.

Mother and I sit on the floor, working the scissors. I use the large Japanese scissors. Mother uses the gleaming silver Western scissors. I slip and cut my middle finger. A red bead of blood forms, then breaks, trickles down. While I suck on my finger, Mother brings a band-aid.

I wrap the band-aid all the way around, squeeze it tightly down. I inhale the odor of the fabric around us.

The smell isn't as strong as naphthalene, but one can tell they've been packed away. They're not damp, of course, but it's kind of like that, this shut-up smell, Mother says, closing her eyes. She breathes in deeply, again and again, exploring the scent.

THE WOMAN TALKED to me. The one who comes and follows.

Lately I have been talking to them, but they rarely come to talk to me.

"It's time you started getting ready," the woman said.

"Ready?" I asked. She seemed unused to speech. That was why her eyes got crossed. Pupils angled toward the center of her face, as when a person tries to focus on the tip of her nose. Eventually they uncrossed. It's eerie talking to a woman with crossed eyes, so I was glad.

"You're going, right?" the woman barked. It's rare, too, for them to bark.

"Where?"

"Manazuru."

I expected this. "What's in Manazuru?" I asked the woman.

"In July, the boat sets out."

"The boat travels across the sea, far, far away," she continued. This time she wasn't hovering in the air, the way she usually did; she stood, the same height as me. We might have been two neighbors, chatting.

"Did Rei go to Manazuru?" Once again, I asked.

"Mm." She was vague about Rei. Perhaps she only pretends not to know.

She seems anxious to say more about the boat. It's a . . . sort of boat . . . waiting at the . . . and brings them in. She speaks in fragments. Her voice sputters at points, it is hard to make out, as though a wind is blowing, making off with the sound.

"Will you go on the boat?" I asked, and again her eyes crossed.

"I won't be on the boat. The boat will go . . . so, no, I can't."

"Does this boat leave, by any chance, at nine at night?" I asked. Tentatively. But the woman made no reply. After her eyes crossed for the second time, it became even harder to catch her words. The wind droned. It wasn't just a feeling, it was really blowing.

"Will you go?" she asked finally, and then she was gone. Blown, perhaps, by the wind.

Will you go? I asked myself. How could I go? I had no idea when the boat would depart, or from what port. And yet I wondered if I would go. To Manazuru, in July.

"MANAZURU WAS A major source of obsidian," Seiji told me.

"You know everything."

"I looked it up. Manazuru is on your mind so much, it's on mine, too."

"In the Jōmon period," he said, "people fashioned weapons and tools out of obsidian. It was a good stone for making tools. I'm sure you learned about it in elementary school."

"I don't recall," I said, and he smiled. It felt odd imagining Seiji looking things up, thinking of me, in my absence. While I was resenting him, just a little, for being unable to be solely mine. Things change. Our relationship evolves.

Lately, Seiji is growing closer. When he gets closer, I need more distance. Or I want us to be as close as we can. The truth is, I don't want it either way. I like it exactly as it is.

"Why don't we go together, to Manazuru," Seiji suggests.

"How about July?"

The woman's words draw me on. Don't pay any attention to the things they say. Only I can't forget, I can't forget.

July. Seiji is thinking. I'll see what I can do with my schedule. Give me some time before I commit, all right? With that, Seiji left. He never hesitates when he leaves. When I get ready to leave, he doesn't want to let me go.

Momo's exams are approaching. June is nearly over. I'm going to the library to study, she says when she gets home from school, and goes back out. Momo's skin looks firmer than it did a month ago. It changes so rapidly. Who is doing this to her? Some person I don't know. A boy, perhaps. Or a girl. The span of my ignorance keeps widening.

Please, Momo, don't let me see the bits I don't know. Preserve my ignorance, Momo.

I think, almost praying.

Momo fluttered her hand and left. I went into my office, leaden.

JULY COMES QUICKLY. More than at the beginning of the year, or at the end, in the middle, time goes too fast.

I think I prefer getting presents I've been anticipating, rather than just being given one all of a sudden, out of the blue.

I remember what she said. I never did learn what she wanted.

Time passes before you get around to asking. July came, bringing with it a ferocious heat. The hydrangea in the garden, the one Mother had tended so carefully, withered. It wasn't only the blossoms that suffered; the stems and the leaves, too, turned brown, and although she watered the plant, and fertilized it, it never revived.

This heat, it's boiling, Momo says. If I get good grades, can I have two summer dresses? This is what she asks for. Is that what you were talking about the other day, what you wanted, dresses? I ask, and Momo shakes her head. No, that was something harder, probably.

Sad when they wither like this, Mother says. I wonder if hydrangeas don't do well in the heat. It doesn't seem hot to me. I'm an old lady, I guess. My senses aren't as keen.

We took a trip, all three of us, to the botanical garden. We packed lunches. Rolled omelets and Spanish mackerel. Beef and *kon'nyaku* noodles boiled in a strong broth. Snow peas. Carrot salad. Rice balls. Momo cooked the snow peas. Don't leave them on too long! Mother cautioned. I know, I know, you boil the water and take them right out. We chattered as we cooked, enjoying ourselves.

At the back of the botanical garden there is a woods. People walk in silence there, avoiding the sun. Momo picked up a large leaf, still green, from the ground. Tiny veins line its surface, vertical ones and horizontal ones.

"They're so detailed," Momo says.

"Detailed? Don't you mean minute?" Mother asks, laughing.

"No, they're extremely detailed." Momo stares fixedly at the face of the leaf. We stop for lunch near the place where she found it. We spread a plastic sheet on the ground, take off our shoes, sit down. I feel the coolness of the earth beneath the sheet. All day long, this place lies in shadow.

My, it's hot, Mother says suddenly.

It's pretty cool here, Momo replies.

Her voice is close, but distant. You're so weird, Grandma, it's much hotter at home. Momo cocks her head. Her voice grows ever more distant. This is dangerous, I think. Dangerous for whom? For Momo? For me? For Mother?

But nothing happened that day. Taking our empty containers and the "detailed" leaf along, we rode the bus home. We were happy, exhilarated, through the night.

MY INSTINCTS ARE seldom right.

So when I felt, that day, a sense of danger, it was probably a coincidence.

Momo disappeared.

She wasn't back by nine, so I ran to the library. It was long closed. I learned, what's more, that it closed earlier, much earlier, than seven-thirty, when she usually returned.

"Library Hours: 9:00 A.M. to 6:00 P.M.," the sign said, clear enough for even a child to understand.

She hadn't been here at all. I understood immediately. For a second, I regretted not having given her a cell phone. Then I changed my mind. Even if she had one, she wouldn't answer if I called. It made no difference.

I hadn't the slightest idea where she might have gone. I ran back home and asked Mother. Well, I don't know, she said, very slowly, where could she have gone? I understood that she wasn't slow, she was petrified. I couldn't ask her for help.

Her friends at school. What were their names?

I couldn't remember, not a single one. Hirose. That's right, Hirose Yukino. They were in the same class in elementary school, took the entrance exams for the same junior high school. I got out the class list, hurriedly rang her.

"I see," Hirose Yukino said, her voice unruffled. Momo probably uses the same tone of voice when she talks to adults she doesn't know. From time to time, she uses it with me, too, and with Mother. I don't know. That's right. No, I can't think of anyplace. Yes. No. Yes. Yes.

Hirose Yukino can't tell me anything. When I hang up the phone, I am at a loss. Telephone the police? Call her teacher? At a time like this, of all times, the woman comes. Vividly, thickly, she follows me.

"Be quiet!" I shout. Mother walks in, frightened. I'm sorry. I apologize. As I apologize to Mother, the woman chuckles.

"Naturally, I know," the woman says.

You know where Momo is! I scream, inside. Say it aloud, and I apologize again to Mother.

"Very close."

Where.

"Come."

I follow the woman. I have a hunch, just maybe, I tell Mother, and run out. The woman is fast. Several times, I nearly lose sight of her. We emerge from the wood that abuts the library, come to the river in the next district. The broad riverbed appears. There is a baseball game going on; the lights above the field are brilliant. The crack of a bat ricochets through the air. The soaring ball parts the night.

Here, the woman says. Past the rows of soccer fields and the baseball field, from a dark expanse of grass, I hear the muffled whining of a dog. I think I can see it, a large black dog, lumbering about. Shrouded in the night, I can't quite make it out.

"Momo," I called.

Ah. There was a small gasp, and beside the dog a slender shadow rose. Another shadow, next to the first, also rose.

"That's you, isn't it, Momo!" I cried, and the slender shadow rocked.

I ran over and clasped Momo to me. She resisted. Stop it, Mom. She pushed me away, hard. The next shadow watched me without moving. Who are you? I demanded, turning to face it. It's none of your business, Momo cried behind me. The shadow retreated, left, just like that. The dog, too. I looked about for the woman, but she, too, had gone.

Only Momo was there, beside me. The heat of the day lingered over the grass.

four

I'M NOT TELLING you.

Was all Momo would say. Who was with you in the field?
However many times I asked, the answer was always the same.
I'm not telling you. I don't want to.

I rebuked her for lying about going to the library, and she
apologized, unexpectedly docile. I'm sorry. I really was at the library until six, though. I did study a little, too.

"A little." The words made my heart brighter, just a little.
Brightening, I was still bewildered. I have no idea, anymore, on
what basis I am scolding Momo. The idea that underage children
should be supervised at all times by their parents? Or that kids
ought to devote themselves to their studies? That young women
must avoid dangerous places? Or is it the platitude, itself smack-
ing deeply of untruth, that people should never lie?

I'm not telling you.

Sitting across from me, Momo holds her ground. So brittle. I
am. As a parent. I was stronger before my husband disappeared.
I scolded Momo, still a baby, without a thought. Right from the
start, I knew when it was okay to scold her, how to scold her. Or
thought I knew.

There was a time when I didn't think about family. Perhaps
this is the same. You only start to think about it when you realize

it is gone. You start thinking, and you no longer understand. You understand less and less.

"Who was it?"

One last time, I ask.

Momo shakes her head. "I won't tell." She replies listlessly. We've been through this so many times, she's weary of it. I begin to feel unjustified, I am bullying her.

"Will you tell me one day?"

I don't know, she replies, her voice barely audible.

She knows. Now Momo knows. I think suddenly.

She didn't know before. But now she does. Poor thing. I had pitied those who don't know. But I was mistaken. Those who know are even more deserving of pity.

I lay my palm lightly on Momo's wiry shoulder. She flinches, just slightly, and I sense that she is allowing my hand to remain there, suffering its weight.

FINAL EXAMS WERE over, the end of the term was approaching. Momo had shot up.

"Look, you're almost as tall as I am," I said to her. And, just like that, Momo drifted away. Unwilling, no doubt, to stand beside me, comparing our height.

"She outgrew me about a year ago, didn't she?" Mother calls from the kitchen.

"Yeah, around then," Momo says, walking into the kitchen. There is a sound of metal rasping against metal. I hear a light ripple of laughter. I can't be sure, with the wall between us, if it is Momo laughing, or Mother. At times like this, particularly, she comes.

"It's almost time," the woman said. She came, hovering, by the kitchen door. The pattern on her clothing is usually blurry, but today it is clear. A sunflower-speckled dress that hugs her body, full white thighs, bare feet, a corn on the joint of one toe, luridly large.

"Time for what?" I ask, and the woman goes cross-eyed.

"The boat, to set out."

"What boat?"

"The boat, I told you before."

Momo and Mother side by side. The curves of their backs, facing me—Momo's slight, Mother's deeply round. I hear, simultaneously, the sound of fine chopping, and water running.

"You're all women here," the woman mutters. She cocks her head, and then, still hovering, twists her hip, stretching the sunflower pattern on her dress.

Because there aren't any boys in this house, Momo said, I remember, when she gave my laptop its name. That Momo is gone now. She is one who was here, but isn't.

What of my husband, then? I don't know my vanished husband, not since he disappeared, the form he would take, and so there is a disjointedness. My husband is not one who is no longer here, he is one who has not yet come.

The not yet come. The one who may, someday, appear.

Only the things we are still holding on to can vanish into the past. If we no longer have it, it can't be lost that way. Can't vanish anywhere. Nonexistent, it is nonetheless unable, forever, to go.

Once again, the woman said, "The boat."

What can I say, I'll go. To Manazuru.

I answered, and the woman vanished. As she vanished, it started raining.

THE RAINY SEASON has ended, yet it is always raining.

Momo is spending her whole summer vacation indoors. Listening, absorbed, to her music. Not out loud, with earphones in her ears, sometimes I hear snatches of rhythm.

Often, she is asleep. She doesn't come when I call her to eat, so I look in her room. She is stretched out, tall, on her bed. Her dark feet poke out from her summer bedspread. "Momo," I call her name, and she turns the other way.

She sure has shot up since summer vacation started. Like a weed, Mother says. Because of all this rain, maybe. Just amazing how she keeps growing.

"I'm going to Manazuru," I tell Mother.

"Oh?" she replies. "Yes, another trip."

"Manazuru feels right to me."

I settled on a day without waiting for Seiji's answer. I called to make a reservation at the guest house with the "Suna" nameplate. Sorry, we're full up that day. It was the man who answered, the son. I called several other inns, but they were all fully booked.

"We've got the festival, you see," I was told when I called a place advertising "seafood fresh from the nets." Finally, I remembered the "beachside resort hotel" where Momo and I stayed. I called. Yes, we have a room. One person. Three nights. Okay. Yes.

The hotel was a distance from the port, perhaps that explained it. The ease with which I got a room. You're going for four days? Mother said. It wasn't a rebuke, not quite, but her tone had a critical tinge. Yes, four days. I'm sorry. My response sounded a shade sharper than I intended.

Three women living alone: it was getting oppressive. I had never left the house for so long, three nights, four days. Not once since Rei disappeared and we moved in with Mother.

No need to be so solemn, Mother says, half laughing. Poor thing, she's thinking. My poor daughter. Poor Kei.

The rain outside made the floor darker. My eyelids felt heavy.

THE RAIN CONTINUED into the morning, then it let up.

On the Tōkaidō line, seated on the left side, one elbow propped on the windowsill, I watch for the ocean that flickers into view, from time to time, between mountains, between houses.

It glitters. It looks like fish scales, layer upon layer. See you when you get back, Momo said as I was leaving. Lately when I talk to her, more so even than before, she looks away, annoyed. My fingertips go cold. When she ignores me. It's true, I'm brittle. I feel it every time, as I go cold. Still I find Momo adorable. Testy, but adorable.

Her voice echoes in my ear. See you when you get back. As the train barrels on, I feel a lightness in me. Emotionally, physically, I am cleansed. What ever inspired me to have a child? Before I gave birth to her, I never suspected it would be like this.

It is impossible to get away. I must shoulder it. "Shoulder" is too grand a word, but that only makes it harder. In a sense, Momo is shouldering me. Things are vague, unsettled.

"If things were settled, you wouldn't have the energy," the woman said.

Startled, I glanced around. She was just outside the window.

"You're fast," I said, and the woman smiled.

"It's not as if I'm running alongside the train."

"Oh."

My emotions become indistinct. I glimpse the sea through the woman's semi-transparent form. It glitters. Momo, I love you, I think suddenly. *Love* can't express it all, but I know no other word that will, and so I repeat it, once more, to myself. *I love you.*

"You're too wrapped up in your daughter," the woman tells me.

Be quiet! I shout, in my mind. The woman laughs. Then she moves away, disappears into the ocean. The surface of the sea sparkles all the more brilliantly, all the way to the horizon. The next stop will be Manazuru, Manazuru, the announcement says.

No sooner had I arrived at the hotel, hung up my clothes, and tossed my body down on the bed than a wave of tiredness came over me. Thinking that I should turn down the air conditioner, I drifted smoothly off to sleep.

When I come to, it is evening, and the sky is on fire. I must have slept for more than two hours, but my body refuses to wake. I go out onto the veranda and listen to the roaring of the waves. It is a wild sound. The wind, too, is strong. I turn on the television, and the newscaster keeps repeating the word "typhoon."

I wash my face, redo my lipstick, get ready to go out. I haven't dined alone for a while. Alone, I walk the roads Momo and I walked together last time. The wind teases with my hair. I feel forsaken.

Over time, I have come to feel forsaken. I didn't used to feel this way. I was fine. On my own, with another person, with many people, I was fine, always. Not now. I can't get used to it. My body can't get used to it. Being alone, being three, as soon as I feel I have finally grown accustomed to the atmosphere of a given moment, someone steps away, or joins the group, and the air changes; it takes time for me to get used to the change.

I sit on the beach and peruse Rei's diary. Boats return from the offing. Where could they have gone, on such a windy day? "Lost a little weight." From time to time, this appears.

Was he gradually losing weight, in those days? I don't remember that at all. I do remember the bathroom scale. The small apartment where Rei and Momo and I lived, the three of us, I would vacuum twice a day, it was so small it wasn't a problem. Momo constantly tracked in sand and mud.

The scale had an orange rim, it was padded with cork. A couple, Rei's friends, gave it to us for our wedding. Rei despised it.

"Why?" He grimaced when I asked.

"C'mon, a scale? It's so cultured, so hoity-toity."

You're an odd one, I laughed, and he said, Look, don't laugh at me. *Look, don't laugh at me.* How I warmed to those words. Innocently, carefree, I warmed. Back then, ages ago.

I think the word: *sickness.* Was Rei sick? He fell ill, felt his death approaching, disappeared? No, I thought, sometimes, it's too cruel. At other times, I wished it were true.

Either way, it is pitiful to be left behind. True, but who deserves more pity, the one who leaves, or the ones who are left behind? the woman asks. I don't even want to think about it. I reply coldly. The woman vanishes quickly into the sea. The instant before she sank from view, slipping under the waves, her feet gleamed, white.

I ROSE LATE the next morning. The previous night, I had eaten a light dinner and gone to sleep by ten. I felt as if I could sleep forever. Just like Momo.

Thinking I might hear the sounds of the festival, I stepped out onto the balcony, but there was only the pounding of the waves. The hotel stood a good way in from the road, so I didn't hear any cars, either. I had coffee for breakfast, nothing else, and rode the bus to the port.

Where does the festival take place? I asked a middle-aged clerk in front of a liquor shop. The port was crowded, more than when I'd been there last, but it hardly looked like a festival.

"Oh, at this hour they've probably still got the *omikoshi* moveable shrine up on the mountain, out in front of the shrine itself," she drawled.

I looked for the woman, but she wasn't around. Completely useless, I muttered to myself, and immediately she appeared.

"You come if I call you, I see," I said.

"Pure coincidence," the woman answered without smiling.

The festival is just beginning, I guess, I said, and she nodded. We turned our backs on the port, entered an alleyway. Soon the ground began to slope upward. On this peninsula, only the area around the shore remains at sea level; beyond that the land slants sharply, rising abruptly to higher ground. The interior of the peninsula is covered, not with mountains, perhaps, but with big hills.

I am out of breath. The woman is fine. She drifts along, following.

"Where are we going?" the woman asks.

"Nowhere. I'm just walking," I reply, and her face clouds over. "What's wrong?"

"I was remembering."

My field of vision dims. A cloud has pushed forward, blocking the sun. Looking at the sky, I see flashes of light in the gaps of the cloud. Soon the cloud passes, it is brilliant again.

"Do you want to go to the cape?" the woman asked. But before I could tell her yes, or no, she was gone.

I looked up again, and was dizzied by the fullness of the light. For a time, I couldn't see.

Rei, I CALLED. To see how it felt.

It was hard to call him by his name, right to his face, but frequently, when he wasn't there, I would say it to myself.

Rei.

Sometimes, too, I would say it to his profile as he lay sleeping. Sometimes I would call out to him during the day, when he was at work, not at home, as I nursed Momo.

The truth is, I have a faint memory of that hour, 21:00.

Three days before he disappeared, having put Momo to bed, I was reading the newspaper at the table. Rei had left it there in the morning when he was done. Slowly I turned the pages, the corners of which, already touched by his hands, lacked the sharpness they had when the paper was delivered. The TV guide, the society section, local news, sports, I read them all, and then I got to the family section.

"HELL." Is what it said. Printed as a headline. I couldn't tear my eyes away.

I don't remember the content of the article. The instant I saw that word, I heard myself calling to him. *Rei.*

In one corner of the quiet living room lay a few blocks, round and square, that Momo had been playing with that evening. The blocks were red, looked like things growing from the floor, and though I knew they meant nothing, they seemed to me like an ill omen.

Rei. I called again. Glancing at the clock, I saw that it was nine, and while every other time I had called him my voice, aimed into emptiness, simply vanished into emptiness, that evening I seemed to hear a voice reply.

Kei.

I heard Rei's voice, weakly, from the living-room ceiling.

Gripped by a sense of foreboding, I folded the newspaper, making a rough, papery rustling. Rei's voice fizzled, and, soon after, the lingering memory of my own voice, too.

Climbing into an alley in Manazuru, I call out, as on that evening. *Rei.*

Sweat from my face bleeds into my eye. I hear the cry of a kite. I'm hungry. I feel my body, and I am relieved. Down an even narrower alley, I find a Chinese restaurant. I rattle the door open on its track. My eyes are unused to the darkness inside. Groping, I pull out a chair, sit.

"WHAT DID YOU have?" the woman asked.

"Wonton soup."

"I envy you."

I walked more after lunch. From alley to alley, from the heights to the low-lying area, my legs ached. Eventually, I got on a bus bound for the tip of the cape. The first time, when I walked, alone, winter had only just ended.

"Get off," the woman urged.

This isn't the last stop, and I'm tired, I told her, and she glared. All right, fine, I said, pressing the button. I stepped down from the bus, and a protected forest spread around me. The growth was thick, hardly any light filtered through the leaves to the road.

You know, says the woman.

You know, somewhere in this great wood, there was a woman who died.

As soon as the woman began speaking, the sky darkened. A deep, gruff rumble came from the distance.

"Thunder?"

"There's a typhoon coming," the woman answered.

I followed the woman as though I were being led along on a rope. A footpath snaked through the great woods, as the woman called the protected forest. As we meandered left and right, I lost track of our direction. Intermittently, gruffly, the thunder continued to boom. The dead woman was strung up in a pine tree. Again the thunder booms. The pine fell down, much later, in a typhoon. The woman tells me, her voice low. The kite no longer cries. Because the wind has shifted, the woman says.

The footpath began to slant downward. The slope steepened, dropping sharply toward the shore. From time to time, I catch sight of waves exploding on the rocks.

"And she was such a good girl," the woman murmurs.

"A good girl?"

"The woman in the tree."

"That's a sickening story, I don't want to hear it," I say, hoping it might help, but it does no good to ask the things that come and follow anything, they won't listen.

"Who'd have thought, to be strung up. Wisteria vines around her feet."

The time between thunderclaps was shortening. Lightning shimmered. The woman held out her hand. Several times, my feet catching in the wet earth, I had almost fallen down. It was cool when I took hold of it. I felt as if I were starting to blur, from the fingertips.

LOOK, SHE PUSHES me. I gaze down at a tidal pool, an enclosure protected by large boulders. The surface of the water is still, even though the waves on the other side, just beyond, are rough.

Isn't it dangerous to be here, if there's a typhoon? I said to the woman, but she didn't listen. The hand linked with mine refuses to let me go. Her grip isn't strong, but I can't loosen it. I've started to blur, I'm numb all the way to my upper arm.

Look carefully, the woman says.

There are tiny fish in the tidal pool, swimming in circles, frantically. Look at them, they're insane, even though they're better off in the shadow of these boulders when the waves are so rough. The woman mutters, laughs. I shudder at how thin, how empty of feeling, her laugh is.

She was spirited away. The girl who was strung up. She was a good girl, really, a darling. She would go early in the morning into the hills to gather firewood, and in the afternoon she would collect clams and seaweed on the shore. At night, she swept, spun. She toiled without resting, and then one day she heard a voice in the woods. Tomorrow, it said, you mustn't go to the hills or the shore.

"But she went anyway?" I asked, and the woman nodded.

She went. And after that day, she was never seen alive again. They searched and searched, and then a fisherman, rowing out to the offing, found her on the ocean.

On the ocean. I didn't get her meaning, so I asked.

"On top of it, not in the water?"

That's right, on the ocean. Reflected there. That same girl. Hair standing on end. She wore nothing but a red robe, an undergarment, wrapped around her waist. Her feet were bound with wisteria vines. Looking up, the fisherman saw her dangling upside-down from a pine branch that jutted out over the water. Her throat and feet were perfectly white.

Thunder rumbles. The lightning is fierce. Waves surge, carrying away the sand. Is that girl you? I ask the woman. No. The woman replies. Is that the truth? I ask again. I don't know, I've forgotten, the woman replies. Thunder crashes. The waves, higher now, can't be held back by the boulders. We'll be swept away, we should move to higher ground, the woman says, gently. I have heard a terrible story, I think, letting the woman lead me. That wonton soup sure was good, I say, intentionally inappropriately, just to see. I've never had wonton soup, the woman says enviously. Lightning and thunder arrive at the same time. There is a tearing sound. With stunning force, the rain begins to fall.

THE RAIN BEAT across the land, omnipresent, yet it felt as if it were directed only at me.

I ran hard, it didn't matter, the rain kept coming. My thin shirt, drenched, clung to my skin.

"You don't get wet," I said, and the woman cocked her head. "I wish I could."

Easy for her to say, strolling on ahead of me, comfortably dry. Even as countless drops of water spill from my head, run down my cheeks, flow from my eyelashes. My white, knee-length skirt is soaked; it has turned a darker shade.

The woman scampers up the stairs on the next hill, opposite the path we descended. I get short of breath following her. Sweat runnels, joining the raindrops.

Arriving at the top, we came to a white building. I remembered seeing it before, when I came by myself. Under all that rain, the building looked abandoned.

"Go on, go inside," the woman said, pointing.

Pushing the glass door open, I was enveloped in warm, close air. My body, assailed by the rain, had grown cold. There were two people sitting dully at the long line of tables; perhaps it was a slow time, between meals. Still, the couple's presence instantly purged the desolate feeling I had carried within me, outside.

Plastic models of the lunch offerings were set out just inside the door. Fried horse mackerel, or sashimi. The waiter walked over, dragging his feet, I asked him for a cup of coffee. You have to buy a ticket from the vending machine, he said.

The woman hadn't followed me inside. The coffee was unexpectedly hot, and my tongue felt scalded. Looking out through the wall of glass that ran from ceiling to floor, I saw pines bending in the wind. The floor was wet from the drops that fell from every part of my body. A small puddle had formed.

I bent down to peer into it and saw, deep down, the woman's face, blurrily reflected.

I NOTICE, SUDDENLY, that there is no sound at all.

Gripping my half-drunk cup of coffee in one hand, I have been gazing down at the woman's face, reflected in the puddle. The size of a bean at first, it grew to walnut size, then finally assumed the size of an actual human face.

The rain still falls. The wind blows. But there is no sound. The voices of the couple sitting at the other table, which I could hear a moment ago, are no longer audible.

From the puddle at my feet, like a geyser bubbling over, the woman gushes forth.

"I'm all wet, aren't I?" the woman asks. She remained dry the whole time we traipsed through the driving rain, and yet now she is sopping. "I've become closer to you, I guess," the woman says with a lovely smile.

Is that why I can no longer hear anything? It isn't only sounds, either, things that were in motion just seconds before have stopped moving. The waiter, the two customers, are frozen, like clay figures.

"The power," the woman said, and immediately the fluorescent bulb over my head began to flicker. Brilliant flashes zigzagged past the window, and suddenly all the lights went out.

"Lightning has struck," the woman explained. In the absence of sound, I had no way of knowing whether it was true or not. All right, come on, the woman beckoned.

Must I follow you, I asked, testing my voice, but it didn't emerge as sound. I realized that when I talked with the woman, it wasn't my real voice; it happened within my body.

Soon the fluorescent bulbs sputtered on, and all at once sound surged into my ears. Mixed in amidst a crush of noise like static from a radio not tuned to any station, but several times more dense, I heard a voice I recognized.

That's Rei, I thought. The sound stopped right away. Only the woman's form was visible, perfectly clear.

Will it be okay, getting back?

Yes, don't worry.

Did the woman ask, or was I the one who posed the question, did the woman answer me, or was I the one who answered her, unable to say, the two of us, indistinguishably intermingled, set out. Lightning bridged the vast distance from sky to ocean, describing a sharp, beautiful line.

Don't worry.

Once again, one or the other of us spoke, and I looked up at the wild sky.

It was a long way here.

So I had thought, but perhaps it wasn't such a long walk, after all.

We plodded step by step along the cement walkway that rimmed the beach, as large waves washed over it. If I hadn't been with the woman, I would have been swept away in seconds, dragged to the bottom of the sea.

"It doesn't end, does it, the rain, the wind," I said, and the woman dimly smiled.

See, the woman pointed back. Even as I turned, the white building was slowly collapsing. For a moment it seemed to have swelled, and then a second later it shriveled, contracting into itself. The building crumbled like a film in slow motion. Not from the roof: the foundation was the first to go. The upper half held its form, the whole roof subsided vertically. Partway down the roof, too, strained and bent, and the next instant everything was massed upon the ground. Dust rose, but the violence of the rain erased it; it too was soon settled.

"The people inside—" I began, and the woman held a long finger to her lips.

"Quiet, keep watching."

As I looked on, obeying, the mound of rubble vanished. Just like that.

"It's gone," I said, and the woman nodded lightly.

"Let's go, onward." The woman twined her fingers in mine. Billows washed over my feet. Some swelled as high as my waist, my shoulders. I was almost gone, but she held me.

"Are we going to meet Rei?" I asked.

"I don't know." The woman is brusque.

We march on and on, tracing the peninsula. Walking, I think of the grumpy waiter and the bored-looking couple I saw in the white building. I wonder if they've all passed on, and the woman shakes her head.

"We're the ones who have passed on." Her tone is flat.

"Momo," I call to the shattering waves. I had forgotten Momo. But I remembered. When I think of her, I feel as though I might be able to make it back. Back where the white building is. Where the woman is not.

The woman tightens her grasp. She blurs into me. An even larger wave comes, and I fade.

I WOKE SHORTLY, and once again felt the rain and wind blowing, everywhere.

"Will we take the boat?" I asked.

"With this storm, the boat won't sail," the woman replies, expressionless.

We were walking at the tip of the peninsula, but somehow we have returned to the port. There is no sign of anyone in festival garb; maybe they are inside, taking shelter from the rain. I do hear the music of flutes and drums, though, coming from far away.

"The sound is back," I say, and the woman shakes her head.

"That's different."

Those sounds are from here, not there, she says, quietly.

I don't really understand the meaning of her words. Oh well, whatever, I say as flippantly as I can, trying. I never intended to come to such a peculiar place.

Oh well, whatever. I could hear my voice. Not an inside voice. It sounded, the way it should, outside me.

"I have Momo, I can't go any further," I told the woman, and her look grew fierce.

"You don't want to meet Rei?" she asked, her voice low.

She does know about Rei, then. I am both persuaded and hesitant.

"Do you really know, really, who Rei was?" I demand of her, my tone sharp, determined not to give in so easily.

"A useless man," she replies instantly.

The wind blows strong. Gusts more forceful than before. The waves are somewhat smaller in the port, but beyond it they pound with strength enough to erode the breakwater. Was he, really, a useless man? I wonder vaguely. My skin is stung by the driving rain.

"Look at you, soaking wet," the woman says with a sneer.

It's true, I realize, my body, not only the outside, but the interior, too, is wet. Without thinking, I crouch down, making my body round.

MOMO, I CALL her name. Help. Help me, Momo.

"You'd ask a child for help?" The woman jeers. Such merciless laughter, I think to myself. What does she know, she's never even had wonton soup.

I want to strain, build up the blurring places. Tense, make them flood.

No, I say aloud. But the word doesn't sound outside my body.

"You're not really unwilling, at all," the woman insists. Her tone annoys me. Why did she, a woman like her, have to come to follow. "You're just like me."

That's not true, I shake my head. The woman never ceases jeering. I scatter the blurring, try to return to what I was, but I can't. Gradually the flooding starts. More than when I coupled with Rei, more than when I couple with Seiji, without resistance, I flood.

During Momo's birth, I was told, Don't push. The cervix had dilated enough already, even now the fetus was on its way out, gradually revolving, and yet—

"Don't push."

They told me, sternly. Endure. It's too early. It won't be long. But, not yet.

Five minutes' endurance was an eternity. And now, in much the same way, I am enduring. My body yearns unbearably to flood. Cross another line, just one more, focus my strength, close my eyes, concentrate on the core of the blurring, and I will lift instantly to the summit. And yet I don't go.

I remember being told, Don't close your eyes. You can push now. Keep your eyes open. Focus on the ceiling. All right, now tighten your muscles, toward your butt. Push as hard as you can, okay?

Bearing a child is more intense, even, than I suspected. I realized, for the first time, on the delivery table. All the way here, no one ever told me. The word *intense* was, perhaps, a little off. *Strange* might be a better word, I thought. Bearing a child is a strange thing.

I thought, and pushed. I couldn't think at all while I was pushing, but in the instant when I caught my breath, again and again, my mind in a whirl, I thought: *how strange, how strange.*

I had been enduring, and yet I reached the summit. Oh, oh my, a sigh escaped. No sooner had I arrived, than I cooled. At the same time, the woman's form warped. The storm was still raging, but the sounds returned. I was seeing people, too.

The woman went off somewhere. My goodness, look at you, you're sopping wet, let me get you a towel, an elderly lady at a sweet shop called to me. She was a plump old woman, her speech easy, unfazed.

BACK AT THE hotel, I ordered from room service and drank.

A bottle of whiskey, and ice, sure thing. Your room is stocked with beer and so on, in case you feel like a chaser. The voice of the man speaking so smoothly on the other end of the hotel line sounded so real, I could hardly believe it. Where was I all that time? Just before?

An urge to hear Seiji's voice came over me, so I got my cell phone out. I punched the keys, held the device to my ear, but there was no sound. It got soaked in the rain, maybe it's broken. I tried calling home, but again it was silent.

I lift the receiver of the hotel phone, push the buttons. Momo answers. Oh, Mom, it's you. Her voice is gentle. How gently she speaks when I'm away. We exchange a few words, have a conversation. How's Grandma doing? Okay. Is it raining there? It's awful out. Your work isn't done yet? Not yet, I'm sorry. I'll be back the day after tomorrow. Okay. Really? Ah. Yeah.

After I hang up, I dial Seiji's number. But I stop midway. I have the feeling Seiji will intuit it. How, going with the woman, passing on, toward the end, she made me blur.

My face is reflected in a large oval mirror over the chest of drawers. Hair mussed, having been left to dry on its own. Lips without color. Faint shadows had formed beneath the eyes.

I stripped off my blouse and approached the mirror. My breasts hang slightly. My chest is perfectly white. Everything hidden is white. Momo's skin is so much darker. Sometimes I want to touch her skin, so taut it looks as if it has been stretched. But she won't let me touch her anymore. Even though she and I used to be together, talking to each other, walking side by side, one of us falling behind, from time to time, moving ahead, from time to time. I was with her, then, not with the woman.

I see Momo's face through my own. Lately she has come to look like me again. A little while ago, she looked like Rei. Take a bit from her cheeks, push in her eyes, trim her eyebrows, and she would look exactly like me. I hate mirrors, I used to think, all the time. The things that are reflected there, that aren't there. You try to touch your own body, and can't reach it.

I don't hate them anymore. It seems ordinary, now, to have a body. When I was Momo's age, my body was more than I could understand. I didn't know which parts of my body worked in what ways, which parts responded how. And in my ignorance, I was afraid.

Who was Momo with?

I started thinking back, and grew frightened.

Amidst the rain, a single ray of light pierced the clouds. It struck the mirror, reflected dully. I broke the seal on the whiskey bottle, poured a glass. Tossed it back, straight.

IT WASN'T A dream, or wakefulness either, I was simply listening to the rainfall.

Is it raining in that world? Or in this world?

I saw the woman's face, her lips muttering these words, under my eyelids. But she soon vanished. When I woke, the wind was blowing strong but the rain had let up. The bottle of whiskey, standing on the chest of drawers, was one-third gone. I didn't have a hangover.

I sat up in bed, gazed out the window. I guess I fell asleep with the curtains open. The morning light was shining in, but it was weak. The clouds scudded by. I went down to the restaurant for breakfast. I asked about the festival at the front desk, but didn't understand the answer. They're saying they may do the fireworks tonight. Depending on the weather.

It wasn't the fireworks I was interested in, but I didn't learn any more. I heard there may be a boat going out? Don't know anything about that, the woman behind the counter shook her head, that was all. Mist wafted over the hotel pool. From time to time, a drop of water fell from the edge of a beach umbrella standing open by the pool. Water had collected on the white tables, and on the white chairs.

Maybe that person with Momo was Rei.

The thought came to me last night. I had no reason to think so. Momo had been relaxed, but also seemed uneasy; if I wanted a clue, that was all I had to go on.

Oh my, I shook my head. What am I doing here, in such a place? How many times have I come here? Thinking. I should pack my things and go home, now. I have work to do.

The woman came.

"Apparently the boat may not set out today, either," she said gruffly.

"Because of the typhoon?"

"Yes."

She sat on the floor, her feet out. Her skirt hitched up to her thighs, revealing her swollen veins. "Have you ever given birth?" I asked.

"I have," the woman answered.

"To how many?"

"Seven."

That many? Seeing my surprise, the woman assumed a vaguely supercilious air. Three boys, four girls. Two of them were twins. The third boy was really a twin, too, but the other one was stillborn. The girl twins grew up good and healthy.

There was a writer who had two sets of twins, Yosano Akiko, I think, I said, curious how the woman would react, but all she did was gape.

Akiko? What are you talking about? the woman muttered.

Beside the white building that had collapsed yesterday, there stood a stone inscribed with a poem by Yosano Akiko. It remained standing, solitary, even after the building fell. So what happened to the building? I asked the woman.

"It's still there, same as always," the woman replied.

So was all that an illusion?

What strange questions you ask. The woman laughed. You're asking *me* whether or not it was an illusion?

I laughed, too, my voice joining hers. True. It is kind of strange. *Strange.*

"Where are your children now?"

"I have no idea." Once again, she turned gruff.

The boat may not set out, but there will be a Kagura dance. For the god. It's a nice festival, it really is, done by the locals, she says, sounding like a tour guide.

Tell me more about Rei. Tell me, please? I moved my face closer to the woman's. She turned, drew back. I thought she would vanish, but she didn't vanish, she just fell silent.

By the time I finished breakfast, the mist had deepened.

I HEAR A woman crying.

The festive mood is more apparent today than it was yesterday. Since morning, men have been weaving through the town carrying posts decked out, umbrella-like, with paper flowers. People beating drums and playing flutes, packed into the long, narrow bed of a beautifully decorated truck, lead the way for the *omikoshi.*

From time to time, mixed with the music, I hear the woman crying. Or maybe it is the wind moaning. Yes, it was only the wind, I think, relieved, and the next instant I begin to think again that it is the woman crying.

The tone of the flutes and drums is bright. The woman's crying is dark. Sometimes I lose sight of the flower-covered posts, the shrine moving along. The mist is thick. I make my way forward, relying on the sounds, then my field of vision expands, once again I am in the midst of the bustle.

"She was a good girl, a good girl," the woman says, crying.

"What girl?"

"The girl strung up in the tree."

It wasn't you, was it, it was your daughter? I ask the woman, but I can't see her, I feel as if I am all on my own. Without her expression before me, I am at a loss.

"I don't know." There is only her voice.

Why would anyone want to have children? Dogs do, and cats, foxes, deer, people. When my heart turns to Rei, when it turns to Seiji, it is utterly unclouded, it is only when my heart turns to Momo that it is overcast, everywhere. I'm as confused as in my youth, when I didn't know how my body worked and how it responded. I have no idea how my heart turns to Momo, in what way it reaches toward her, whether it is affection or dislike, love or hatred, or to what extent they are commingled.

"It's easy if they're not your children, when they belong elsewhere," I murmur, and then, slowly, the woman's form emerged from the mist.

"Really? Is it really so?" the woman asked.

Maybe not. I laughed, and she did, too. I am glad she has stopped crying. I feel pity for a crying woman.

"Look at me, I'm all wet again." The woman held out her arms. A fine rain falls and stops, stops and falls, intermittently. The drops don't roll from the woman's skin, they seep into it.

"We've become very close, haven't we," I said, and the woman nodded.

"Take care," the woman said, walking behind me.

Of what? I asked, turning around, but by then she was gone. I felt a sense of disjointedness in the center of my body. A terrible pain seized me, just below the pit of my stomach.

"Lost a little weight." I remembered the words in Rei's diary. I wrapped my arms around my body, embraced myself. Held myself, strongly, in my arms.

five

I T'S LISTING, I thought. And then, just like that, the boat keeled over.

Countless people, thrown overboard, sank.

It was filled beyond capacity. Earlier in the afternoon, in the aftermath of the typhoon, the wind had still been strong. Yesterday, the boat had not gone out. Today, toward sunset, when the wind died down, the decision was made that this passage should take place.

There were many times more people at the festival than the day before. The crowd swelled so fast it was as if the earth had disgorged them. Stalls lined both sides of the street; the smell of sauces charring on iron griddles hung, heavy, thick, in the air.

Musicians, playing their flutes and drums, alone had filled the boat; then, *happi*-clad men, clambering over each other, boarded as well.

"Why do they hurry so?" the woman asked. Since nightfall, her presence had grown strong again. It was more than her presence; often her form appeared to me, clear as day.

"You keep coming and going," I said. She smiled thinly.

"Because you keep calling me back," she replied. "Because you insist."

She says I insist. But it is not true. I do not need this woman following me.

"Why do they hurry so, those men," she sneered. "Toward death?"

Human forms, thrown in an arc from the deck when the packed boat lost its balance, rocked among the waves. In the swath where darkness lay against the ocean, many heads popped indistinctly into view, then vanished—vanished, then reappeared.

"It's shallow enough, they won't die," I said.

The woman nodded.

"They will, eventually," she muttered.

The boat exposes its belly. As it rolls, upends itself, human heads surface, roiling up from beneath it. It is like some brilliant, gleeful game that people play in the shallows, near the shore, where there are no waves. And yet out there, down below the capsized boat, bodies may be plunging, arrow-like, into the depth.

"Will any of them, out there, die?" I ask the woman. "I mean, here, right now?"

"I couldn't say." She is brusque. As always.

Among the heads bobbing on the waves are arms flung toward the sky; other forms appear to be treading water. People are still there, in the water. Slowly, the capsizing of the boat comes to seem like just another highlight of the festival.

A huge firework is launched from the shore. And the boom follows.

THE BOAT ONTO which the moveable shrine has been loaded, however, surges on, leaving the upended hull in its wake, and beaches below the main shrine.

The shrine is taken ashore. The men transporting it, themselves transported, voices raised, lug it on their shoulders up the steep incline to the shrine at the top of the hill.

Buffeted by the crowd, I am pulled farther from the foundering boat. The flow carries me to the foot of the stairway to the shrine. I cannot resist.

Wait, I call to the woman. Just now, her presence faded. One body after another streams past me, each face flushed with the thrill of the festival. I am surrounded by people, and yet, bit by bit, I cease to feel them. They are nothing but the heat of things around me.

I push my way free of the stream. I collide with many human bodies. Their hands and feet knock against me, like hard balls. I dart into a narrow alley, and breathe. I look around, but there is no sign of the woman.

I walk uphill. The alley opens out into a clearing. A vine wraps around the rotting pillar of an abandoned house. The weeds reach my knees. Dozens of sea stones lie scattered among the grasses. Up here, there is nothing of the commotion below.

"Quiet, isn't it, when you get a little higher up," the woman says.

I am caught off guard. When did you come back? I ask, and she says, I never leave.

Seated on a rock in the clearing, I peer at the ocean. I can see only a narrow strip of water along the wall of a rundown storehouse that stands, off to one side, before me.

One after another, fireworks soar into the air. They make no noise. I realize, suddenly, that there is no sound at all anymore. Just like yesterday, when I stopped for coffee in the white building on the cape.

There, look.

The woman points. The upside-down boat nudges into the strip along the storehouse wall, drifting slowly in the water. A shower of sparks rains down across its belly. Soon the sparks become small flames that begin to hop and weave around the hull like will-o'-the-wisps. The wet wood starts to burn, then goes out. Then begins burning again.

At last the boat catches fire.

"It's caving in," the woman says.

Slowly, very slowly, the boat dissolves into flame. The people, too, pitching among the waves, are consumed, gracefully, quietly, by the inferno. They seem so tiny, the boat so bulky, as they are absorbed by the fire.

"Beautiful, isn't it?" the woman murmurs, forlorn.

I WALK IN a place without sound.

A strong wind is blowing. Earlier, toward sunset, it had died down, I am sure it did, but now the gusts assail me continually, right and left. Occasionally a whirlwind rises. My hair clings to my face. Shutting my eyes, I seem to feel drops hitting me. Does it hurt? the woman asks. No, I'm okay, I reply. And she takes my hand in hers.

She leads me, and I walk.

I hear nothing, I see nothing. My eyes are wide open, and yet there is no scenery. I might be wandering through a thick fog, or drifting woozily within myself, lost in a deep trance. Off in the distance, there is the surface of the ocean, the burning boat.

"Dreadful, isn't it." The woman says this every so often, turning to look.

"Did they all die—in the fire?" I ask.

She does not answer. After all the—, she begins.

After all the what?

After all the trouble they went to, she says, finally, launching the boat.

All at once, ahead of me in the fog, there is a party of men, marching forward. Something about their backs suggests that they are embarking on a journey. The men are wrapped snugly in their coats, they carry leather traveling bags. Their hair is neatly combed. In their breast pockets, no doubt, are crisp, new tickets.

"Rei," I call.

One of the men turns.

But it is not Rei. The next man looks back as well. He has handsome chiseled features, he reminds me of Rei, yet he has none of Rei's energy. The next man in line turns around. Like grass stirring in the wind, one after another, the heads swivel: one male face after another reveals itself.

Rei's is not among them.

The woman still leads me by the hand. Let go, I say, hoping it will work, but she does not let go. I want to dash over, cry out Rei's name, find him, but I cannot.

"Were they on the capsized boat?" I ask.

I don't know, the woman says, and pulls my hand, hard. I nearly fall. Without meaning to, I cry out. All at once, again, the men turn.

That's Rei, I think. All the way up front, among the undulating backs of the walking men, his face appears, is hidden, emerges again. His features are the same as when he disappeared, in his mid-thirties.

Beside myself, I scream his name.

But this time no one turns.

The boat is burning. Pale white smoke climbs, breaking apart into innumerable lines, from the area around the port, far below.

Rei, I think, strongly. No matter how strongly I think, he will never return. I know that. I know he will not be coming back. And yet I can't help thinking, so strongly.

ONCE AGAIN THERE is no one else, only the two of us, alone.

How far have we walked, I wonder. We are standing on an unfrequented bit of shoreline. This is not the port near the market, where the men carried the shrine and the posts all decked out with paper flowers; there is no one, nothing in sight, but the quay, dark, partly submerged beneath the waves.

"I've been here before, to this beach," the woman says.

Before, when? I ask offhandedly. The woman no longer pulls me by the hand. She stands, lost in thought, facing the sea.

After I had the twins, she tells me.

The woman appears now, cradling one twin in her arms, with the other on her back. It is more than her presence; I hear a baby crying, faintly, too.

"You came to see the ocean?"

"I saw the ocean every day."

"Did you come to feel the wind, then?"

"The wind, too, I felt every day."

"So what did you come for?"

Sometimes I got sick of living, the woman snapped. Harried with work all day long, morning to night, without even realizing how haggard I had become, no idea of the things that make me happy, having no contact with the depths of people's hearts, never even realizing that my own heart had its depths, too, simply counting the minutes, oh, it all got so tiresome.

The woman tossed the baby in her arms into the ocean. She untied the twisted cords that crossed her breast, binding the second baby to her back, clasped her once to her bosom, then tossed her away, too. The babies floated for a moment on the tide before the ocean swallowed them.

The woman changes. Now she is wearing a white pants suit, and holds a black square bag. You've had wonton soup, I'm sure, looking like that. I think to myself. A few strands of hair have broken free from her bun, at the base of her neck, and turn lightly in the wind.

"I was always like that, sick of it all," the suited woman says.

Perhaps, but Rei wasn't sick of anything. I fire back, speaking the words only in my heart. Even these utterances of the heart communicate immediately to the woman. That Rei of yours, a useless man. The woman snickers. She said the same thing yesterday. A useless man. Without even knowing him.

Useless or not, once he's gone, you can't help it, left behind.

The wind whips around the woman. Wonton soup, *jiajiang* noodles, whatever you feel like, we can eat them together. Don't talk anymore about being sick of it all, let's just live our lives, effortlessly, without a thought. I call to the woman, once again, in my heart.

She shakes her head in disbelief. Are you for real, or a flake? I don't get you.

For real, flaky—like they can be separated. We're alive, you know! I shout at her.

The woman falls silent; the wind keeps whipping around her.

I WANT TO go home. I think.

The smoke from the burning boat has drifted this far. It is a gray mist, filling the sky.

Why do they all hurry so, to go? To sink down, into the ocean? I ask the woman, but she has not been present for some time. I am all alone here now.

I have no choice, I start to walk. Walking on, alone, I think of Rei.

We went to see a waterfall. It was before we were married. The waterfall was deep in the mountains, at the end of a road too narrow for the car. The spot where the cascade commenced its fall was so high we could not see it. The sunlight was strong. It cut into our eyes. There was no hope with that sunlight, even less, of discovering the point from which the water fell.

"It's kind of creepy, not knowing where the water comes from," I remarked.

And Rei agreed, Yeah.

A moment passed in silence. Then:

"Do you know where you come from?" he asked. "Kei?"

Me? Where I come from? I repeated, unsure of his meaning.

Rei nodded, slowly.

Actually, he began, my first memory is very vivid. I was three.

Oh, that's what you meant, by where I come from, I said, cocking my head, and Rei put his arm around my shoulders, drew me closer. Chilly, isn't it? he asked, simply.

I was three years old, and I was trying to grab this bug from a tree in the garden. It was green, sort of a peculiar shape, long and thin. Only I couldn't control my grasp, so I couldn't really pick it off, I ended up grabbing it with my whole hand, and all of a sudden goo squirted out of the bug's body. All over my palm, all sticky. I just squashed it.

So I went in with it, like that, to where my mother was, in the kitchen, and showed her my hand. She drew back from me. I knew it wasn't me, it was the bug she was avoiding, but still it hurt me. The bug wasn't alive anymore. I hurled it down on the floor. The bright green of its body was very clear, I remember, against the floor's deep wooden hues.

That's a walking stick, my mother told me. You don't see them often.

I'd never heard that name, walking stick, before. My mother didn't back away again, she lifted the bug between her fingertips, her expression perfectly ordinary, and then she opened the kitchen door and tossed it out into one of the plants in the garden.

I wanted to get the juice off my hand, so I went over and rubbed my palm back and forth on the earthen floor just inside the door, in the entryway before you step up into the kitchen. I could see my mom, a shadow, looming overhead. She stared at me, very still.

"I've never seen a walking stick," I said, and Rei smiled slightly.

So that's where I come from, that scene with the walking stick. That's where I begin. Like the waterfall, coming from up there. I have no memory of anything before that. Even though it's my life, he said, and pulled me closer, stronger, against him.

"I don't really know where I come from," I told him. Chilly, isn't it, he repeated. It wasn't winter. I can't remember whether it was early spring or late autumn. I always forget these things. I've forgotten, even, where I come from.

The waterfall kept cascading down, ever new, like something that had only just appeared, sending up clouds of spray. Even though it had been falling there for centuries.

IT'S TRUE, IT is, I'm always forgetting. I've forgotten a good deal about Seiji, too. Since I came here. To Manazuru.

Even as I walk on, alone, Seiji is not in my thoughts. Poor thing, I think. But what am I thinking? Is it Seiji I pity? Or do I pity myself, for not thinking of him?

The boat is still burning. I have left the sad, unfrequented bit of shoreline, and once again I am approaching the port. There is a bitterness to the smell of fire. There is a touch of bitterness, too, in Seiji's breath. Something acrid within the sweetness. When we embrace, saliva passes abundantly between us. There, too, there is a bitterness.

At times, it is not Seiji who embraces me, but I who embraces him. It is not a question of how it happens, it is a feeling, how the air hangs in the room, the coolness of our skin.

Sometimes, embracing Seiji, I recall Rei, telling me where he is from. I do not know where I come from, but there are moments when I begin to remember the odors of the place, faint sounds that reached me, the loneliness.

Rei drew me in, but with Seiji I can remain just as I am, endlessly, drifting. I am not lonely. Whether it is he who embraces me, or I who embraces him. And so, all the more, I remember the old loneliness.

"You look so forlorn," Seiji tells me.

So I look even more forlorn. I do not mean to, but I am pulled back, deeper and deeper, into the lighthearted loneliness of the time, long ago, before it all happened, before I met Rei, when I knew nothing of the world beyond the cradle of my parents' hands.

I come to the port. There is no one left from the festival now. Only the music boat, still burning. Reduced to a white skeleton, the hull still smolders, riddled with small flames.

Overhead, I hear a helicopter. Sound has returned, I think, and suddenly the landscape regains its color.

I don't want to go back. Was it this that Rei felt? No desire, maybe, to go back. Still caught in my uncertainty, the agony of it, in a flash, I have returned.

REACHING THE HOTEL, I pick up my key and go out to the pool. The pool is outside the lobby. Ripples drift across the water's surface. I had thought the air was still, but there is a breeze.

I sit down under a beach umbrella. The plastic table creaks when I lean my elbow on it. The woman's presence is thick.

We've become very close, haven't we? I had said to her.

The colonial-style ceiling fan in the lobby rotates in slow, broad circles. The surface of the pool gleams in the light from the lobby. Sometimes I see the figure of a dead man in the water. No, he isn't dead, he's been thrown into the ocean, that's all. The men came up onto the beach right after that, dripping.

The woman tells me, whispering in my ear.

At 21:00, Rei was with a woman I had never seen. I had forgotten that, all along. But now I have remembered.

So they didn't die, those men. What about the boat, the one on fire? I ask the woman.

It was never on fire, of course not, she replies. It just capsized, that's all. It would never burn that close to the shore, people aren't going to die. Don't be ridiculous.

But I saw it happen.

Maybe you wanted it to happen.

No, I didn't. I deny it, and then, all at once, I am clutching my stomach. The pain is back. The woman Rei was with was lovely. She looked slightly younger than me. She wore her hair up, revealing a mole on her neck. A mole one wanted to reach out and touch.

There was a splash from the pool, and for a moment light filled everything. I was dazzled, blinded. Rei squeezed the woman's hand. The woman squeezed back, gently. They were talking. I couldn't hear. They were too distant for me to hear. But I saw the intimacy of their words. But I had forgotten. All along, I had forgotten.

Did you really? the woman asks. Her tone is ruthless.

Had you really forgotten?

The pain is fierce in the pit of my stomach. The light off the pool is almost too much to bear, it has become so strong.

THE NIGHT DEEPENS.

The hotel is full of sounds. The rushing of the waves. Trucks driving in both directions on the dark highway. The night receptionist settling wearily into his creaky seat. Countless winged insects buzzing by, just outside my window.

I let my head sink into the pillow, try to remember. What I had forgotten. What I have been trying to forget.

Rei's voice, calling my name, Kei. Every time he said it, something in my body ached. Like a dull blade, his voice hurt. I loved him so intensely, helplessly. I was captivated by him. I had believed that if we married, if I bore his child, in our life together, whatever a life together was, I could dilute the fierceness of my fixation. But I was unable to.

The woman's profile was white. Perhaps they were meeting on business. An appointment at 21:00. The hour, scribbled on a scrap of paper. The evening Rei met the woman, he wore a dark green jacket. The woman wore soft clothing. Everything about her, her clothing, her hair, seemed to be pulled in Rei's direction. Like seaweed on the river bottom.

I had followed Rei. I left Momo with Mother, got a seat near dusk in a café near his office, and waited. It was after eight when Rei came out of the main entrance. He went straight down into the subway. I dashed out of the café, tumbled down the steps after him. Rei swept through the gate with his pass. I hurried after with the ticket I had bought in advance. I had prepared tickets for the subway, the JR train lines, and the private line a short walk from his office—every possibility. Kind of an odd occasion to be so thorough. I seem to hear the woman's voice. But it was not the woman's voice. It was my own.

Rei stepped into the train. I got on the next car down. I felt the rocking of the train, to and fro, very strong. My body swung heavily in time. I watched Rei, clandestinely, where he stood, next to the doors connecting the cars. He stood with his back straight, swaying.

I noticed my pale face reflected, thin, distorted, on the silver handrail.

THAT TWISTED FACE was my own, without a doubt, and yet, suddenly, it was another.

Ah, I gasped.

It was then. The first time one came, clearly, and followed me.

I couldn't tell for sure whether the reflected face was a woman's or a man's, but the expression was utterly different from my own; it was nothing more than a reflection on the silver handrail, and yet the way it stared out at me, its frozen gaze, stopped me.

"It's two, overlapping," I murmured.

My own face and a stranger's, doubling, more twisted than before.

The train rocked violently.

I looked at Rei. The back of his dark green jacket was slightly curved, and he was gazing out the window into the darkness. An air of fatigue tinged his profile. He was only a little distance away, and yet we were not together.

Rei got off at the second stop. I followed, mingling with the crowd. The distance between us grew, then shrank, shrank and grew, and when the rush of people pressed me near enough that I could have reached out and touched him, I almost called out, Hey.

He wouldn't turn, even if you did.

The thing that followed whispered into my ear. No, I know, I replied, silently.

On and on, Rei kept going. To where the woman was. To meet the woman with the mole on her neck. I could have stretched out my hand, he would never have noticed, a cool, thin wall standing between us, that was how it was.

The woman was waiting.

The moment Rei and the woman were seated across from each other, the air around them filled with light. I couldn't see, it was so bright.

IT WAS A hotel lounge.

A tall glass stood before the woman. Light green, a cocktail, she took only the smallest sip before setting it back down.

When she let go of the glass, she looked hard at Rei.

Rei did the talking. He didn't take any papers from his brief-case, there were no explanatory gestures punctuating his conver-sation, it hardly looked like work, it was very intimate.

Rei ordered a drink, as well. I stood motionless in the spa-cious lobby just off the lounge. The revolving door turned slowly, and everyone who entered or left passed by me.

After a time, a dish and a glass were brought out. Rei pushed the dish, which had been set down before him, forward, to the center of the table, midway between him and the woman. The woman reached out a hand. She deftly fingered a small, thin thing and raised it to her lips. She wiped her fingers on her nap-kin. Next, Rei reached for the plate. He seized a larger clump of something, lifted his hand straight to his mouth. The woman was watching. How he touched his lips lightly to his fingers, how his lips moved as he chewed.

The lobby offered a clear view of the lounge. Rei was in a flat, open place. The woman sat between us. Suddenly, hatred filled me.

My body pulsed with it, until my legs shook. I walked over to a sofa in the lobby, and sank my body into it. Rei and the woman were now only half visible. But the sense of their presence reached me, thick. I thought I could hear their voices. Even though I knew I was too far away to hear anything.

"Rei," the woman is saying.

Rei speaks the woman's name. What is her name? His lips move, softly.

"Rei," the woman says again.

Rei toys with her hand, without replying.

I couldn't hear them, yet I felt as if I could. I couldn't see them, but I felt I could.

Madam, I heard a voice. From a distance, on the other side. I kept looking down, and the voice came again. Madam.

Glancing up through my disheveled hair, I saw a man in a hotel uniform. Are you feeling unwell? Would you like me to bring you a glass of water? he asked.

I shook my head, briskly looked up. No, thank you. I'm fine, really. The uniformed man bowed slightly. I'm glad to hear that, excuse me for interrupting, he said, and turned away.

"Rei."

The woman's voice echoed through the room. It didn't, but I felt as if it had.

"So what did you do?" the woman asks.

I forget, I reply. We are in the midst of the commotion, in Manazuru. Funny, the festival should be over by now, I say to the woman, and she shakes her head, amused. It takes very little to send us back.

A moveable shrine passes by. Men in *happi*, headbands twisted around their heads, sending beads of sweat flying every which way. The shrine bobs up and down with their movement. Several shrines, each from a different part of town, go up and down the street, competing.

There is a band of musicians on a truck, playing flutes and drums. They are in time, in tune, they keep playing on and on, over and over, the same melody, it seems it will continue forever, and the woman is at my shoulder, eyes closed, entranced.

"You haven't forgotten," the woman whispers. Her voice is so quiet it should be drowned out by the noise, but I hear her perfectly clearly.

Did I, not forget? Rei, and the woman, stepping side by side into the hotel elevator, I was unable to follow them where they went, the two of them, alone, together, so I simply stared at the number marking the floor they ascended to, it wasn't one of the top floors where the bars and restaurants are, neither was it one of the lower floors where all the banquet halls are, the number where it stopped was in the middle, where the guest rooms are, it stayed lit up for a while before it moved again, is it possible, could I really have seen all that?

"Maybe you did," the woman whispers, looking me in the eye.

I turn away, and think of Momo.

I never saw it. I never saw anything like that. It was just something I imagined. Something that took root in me, ballooned in me, like a summer cloud tearing, changing shape, becoming round, and then, before you know it, growing long and thin at one end, tearing again into little shreds, it was like that, a sort of obsession that filtered through a gap in my thoughts, that kept shifting, expanding, shrinking, assuming the most frightening forms, then suddenly becoming a brightly shining thing, that's all it was, really, I'm sure of it.

Next year, I'll bring Momo for the festival, I think. How much of that memory is real, how much isn't, perhaps all that was something that never was, right from the start, and yet I've committed it all to memory, so clearly, from beginning to end, maybe that's all this is, the festival keeps moving on, shining, next year, definitely, Momo and I, standing side by side, drinking in the power of the festival around us—

"Don't get carried away." The woman bars my way.

Blocked, I feel myself tumbling to the bottom of a hole.

It strikes me, suddenly, that my body is growing faint. Just like this woman, following me. There is sadness in the woman's voice. Momo, I think. Momo is, adorable. Momo is, adorable, to me. I think, growing fainter. The posts decked out with paper flowers, and the men around them, fan out in a wide circle partway up the hill, and dance.

I WENT ON like that, following the woman's lead, deeper in.

I found myself, not knowing how, at the end of the path I had climbed, in the open space, leaning on the pillar of the abandoned house. The ocean visible through the gap.

"No sound, again," I say, and the woman nods.

When the sound ceases, it seems a space has opened up around me. Any number of them come to follow, no one I recognize. They have a slight heaviness, more than the fainter ones that gather in department stores, but their forms, innumerable, remain unclear.

"Leave them alone, they'll go," the woman says.

I nod. Yes, I know. I know that very well.

There was another time, too, when I saw Rei and the woman together.

At night. There's a farewell party tonight, so I'll be late, Rei said. Momo and I ate dinner early. We bathed together, and I put Momo to bed. The next morning we were going to field day at the kindergarten Momo would be attending in the spring, so she needed to get to sleep.

We get a lunchbox! Momo was excited at dinner. Again and again, she repeated the words. Lunchbox. Field day.

I want to take a banana, she told me. And a backpack.

You're too young for a backpack. You get a backpack in elementary school, I told her. Momo got mad. Backpacks and lunchboxes, field day, the sandbox, her stuffed rabbit Kiiko, it was all mixed up in her mind. She was very excited.

I want a banana! I want to take a banana! she screamed, at last, in her excitement.

To quiet her, I promised her a banana. After I tucked her in, I ran to a supermarket that was open late. My hair, freshly washed, had not yet fully dried. The late summer breeze caressed my skin, faintly warm.

I saw them in the shadows outside. Rei and the woman. Huddled, whispering.

"Ah," I said, aloud.

Why, in a place like that. I peered into the darkness. I could see their silhouettes. But as I kept looking, I no longer felt sure that it was him, or her.

I grabbed some bananas. Then a box of tissues. And an apple.

They'll be gone, I thought, if I do some shopping. But when I went back outside, the two figures were still there.

"Hey," I called. It was too hard, as always, to say, Rei.

The larger shadow turned. The light from a streetlamp put his face in darkness. The face, alone, a blind spot. I felt the weight, in my hand, of the bananas and the apple in their white super-market bag.

The two silhouettes stayed there, unmoving.

"WAS IT NICE out, for field day?" the woman asks.

What? I respond.

You went with your daughter, right? To field day?

Well, yes. I guess we did. Momo and I, a banana and the apple in a Tupperware container, a sheet to spread on the ground, we went to the kindergarten, to get a sense of what field day was like, flags of all nations flapping in the wind, around the playground. Yes, I guess we did.

"And Rei. He was there, too." I remember.

It was Sunday. When I woke up, Rei lay asleep beside me, like always.

"Good morning," Rei said brightly.

Momo was still asleep, breathing deeply. We all slept in the same room. Momo to my left, Rei to my right, three futons aligned on the floor like the three vertical strokes of the graph for "river," except the shortest stroke was at the left, not in the middle.

Shhh, I put a finger to my lips, lay my head on Rei's chest. He was about to get up, but he settled back again. I told him, sighing, not speaking, Hold me.

Rei hesitated.

What are you waiting for? I looked him straight in the eye. My face was reflected in his irises. I placed my hand on his pajama pants.

I slipped my hand inside.

Momo sputtered. Her voice and her breathing mixed. Rei remained unmoving, accepting my touch. I lay down on him, my face to his. Like a cover on a futon, two layers, flat. And then I lifted my upper body, moved onto the place where I had set my hand.

Oh, you're inside me, I whispered, and, ever so faintly, Rei frowned.

A pained expression, I thought, moving. It was smooth. Rei shut his eyes, as if he were enduring me. But he was not enduring. Our movements locked right away. Together, like co-conspirators, we moved. Secretly, deeply, without Momo knowing, we achieved our climax.

Momo would get up soon.

I smelled Rei. Tightening myself, I went to the bathroom, I showered. It flowed with the water. I tightened myself again, to keep it from flowing. I wanted him to come inside, deep in my body. To enter the dark, innermost place, to become the form that a person is, originally, this was what I wanted. To make me sick, terribly sick, in the mornings.

Maw-m-my! Momo said, opening the door to the bathing area. I'm going to take a banana, okay? It's nice weather out today, Maw-m-my!

She was still practically a baby, with an adorable, baby voice that made me want to scoop her up, clasp her to me, bury my face in her skin.

AT THE KINDERGARTEN, Rei was distracted. The sunlight burned.

I'm just so tired, I've been so busy lately.

Rei talked, flopping down on the silver-colored sheet we had brought to sit on. He covered his face with his hat, folded his arms behind his head, raised his knees. I could not tell, anymore, whether he was Rei, or some other man.

"Next year, huh," Rei said through his hat, voice muffled. "Kindergarten already."

Momo would be running in a race for incoming students. Hey, I go next, I'm gonna wun! Momo informed Rei, pushing the hat off his face.

Okay, okay, Rei said, and sat up. He lifted Momo onto his lap, slipped his hands under her arms, bounced her a few times. Momo giggled, like bubbles bursting. Mister, me too! Me too! A boy the same age as Momo called nearby, walking over.

No! Momo told him. Hey, Daddy, only me, wight? Only me!

Suddenly I feel uneasy. The sun beats down, strong. I bore Rei a child, we live comfortably together, three peas in a pod, we should be relaxed, settled in our drowsiness, yet the sun is so strong, unpleasantly so, yet it is not the sun that makes me sweat.

A cluster of children, smaller even than the kindergarteners, has gathered for the race. They look lost, unsure of themselves. They grip their mother's or father's hands tightly in their own, their bodies rigid. Momo does not let go of my hand, either, not for a moment.

"Wun with me?" she says forlornly, looking up.

You want me to run with you? Let's try it by yourself, okay? You're a big girl, right?

Momo looks as if she might cry. Rei saunters over. He bends to look at her, smiles. Here we go, he says, lifting her onto his shoulders. On your mark, go! The gun goes off, and still he carries her, surrounded by the bewildered, milling children, walking on.

Perched on Rei's shoulders, Momo's expression is grave. She glances down at the running children, then faces forward again, squeezes her legs tightly around Rei's shoulders, which bob as he walks, and fixes her gaze on a point in the distance.

Well, it looks as though we've got a dad running with us, too! the voice on the loudspeaker says. The director of the kindergarten is providing live commentary. That's it, give it your best, everyone! Let me see each one of you doing your best! He has a gentle voice.

The children run. They move ahead much faster than Rei, as he walks, and arrive in quick succession at the finish line. Rei, unhurried, keeps ambling on, Momo perched on his shoulders.

Don't take Momo from me! I think. Or is it, maybe, Don't take Rei from me!

My heart pounds at our not being, all three of us, together. I break into a cold sweat. It is this sunlight, so strong. Momo comes running. Now that Rei has lowered her from his shoulders, now that they have reached the finish line.

Maw-m-my! Momo yells. Kei, what's wrong? Rei says. I realize, then, that I am crumbling. I lay my body, exhausted, on the sheet, and close my eyes.

"WEAK, AREN'T YOU," the woman said.

Am I? Weak? I asked.

I was still in Manazuru. My body was fainter, the landscape gone, but I could tell, even so, that this was Manazuru.

"Think how lucky you are, you're still alive."

Am I? I guess I am, still alive?

"At least, you're not dead yet, and what a luxury that is."

A luxury, I think vaguely. So is Rei dead, after all?

"You'll never see him again, not if you can't remember."

What's that? I ask. Is he, then, alive?

"Either way, you've got to remember."

She said, that was all, and vanished. Always, always at the crucial moment, she goes.

I begin walking again, utterly exhausted. To the shore, taking a very long time. Stalls line both sides of the road, one after the other. Their lamps flicker.

There is a man. Pressing up against a woman. On the beach, in the shadows. The woman throttles him. The man does not re-sist. So, the woman says, Does it hurt? Is it painful?

It hurts, the man replies. It is Rei's voice. The voice asking, Does it hurt? is mine.

When could I have killed Rei?

The couple in the shadows is soon gone. Next a baby appears. I gave birth to the baby. No, I did not. Rei poured it into me, this child. But then, just after, he disappeared, so I aborted it.

I wavered. He may come back. Just like that. Rei. Half de-spairing, I had hope.

The heat of summer had not abated when he went. The last cicadas were still chirring, and toward dawn, Momo's forehead was always covered with a film of sweat. Field day was in early

September, Rei disappeared in the middle of the month. Without knowing I was pregnant, he was gone.

This child was never born. And yet, there on the beach, distinctly, I see him crawling. The line where his hair meets his forehead reminds me of Rei, his voice is full of strength when he cries, more energetic by far than those late-summer cicadas, there he is, crawling.

There's no baby like that there, I say, imitating the woman's voice. But he does not vanish. My voice resembles the woman's. Inside my ear, it is her voice. Outside, it is my own.

I never killed Rei.

Like a taut string, snapping at the middle, I fling my voice into the darkness.

I am back at the hotel, at the pool. Inside, slowly, the ceiling fan stirs the faintly warm air.

I PRESS MY cheek to the window of the stationary train.

The summer is still at its height, but in another month and a half, autumn breezes will blow, and the stuttering of the insects will have changed beyond recognition. The shrill whine of the cicadas will be gone; the air will fill with the sorrowful chirping of crickets.

Manazuru, I say, aloud.

We glide past the platform, beyond it. I sit in a seat on the ocean side, follow the scenery as it begins to stream away. The rows of houses end, trees appear, the woodland thickens. After a time, we enter a tunnel.

When we leave the tunnel, it is no longer Manazuru. The ocean waves are choppy. A pair of station wagons pass, together, along the road that traces the shore. It seems the waves will wash over their roofs, but they do not. As Manazuru grows more distant, so too do my illusions.

In Manazuru, the two cars would be carried off by the waves as I watched, dragged down to the bottom of the ocean.

Ma-na-zu-ru, I say, and then continue, *To-o-kyo-o.*

The train is a container that ties Manazuru to Tokyo. A container that takes my body from vision to reality, or the other way around, from this world, to the other.

I let myself think of Seiji.

Seiji is in Tokyo. I'll call him when I get to the station. Maybe we can meet, even if it is only for a little while. Within my body, what Rei's body spewed into me, in the vision I had earlier, slowly rocks, back and forth. My fingers remember how they felt closed around his neck. But by the time we reach Kōzu, that, too, will start to fade.

Shuddering, the train speeds on, carrying me, into our world and its time.

six

I OPEN THE SHUTTERS quietly. No one, except me, is awake.
The leaves of the aralia in our small garden grow thick and
vivid; tiny green fruit, very hard, has begun to form on our single
persimmon tree.

I sit down and stare.

I wanted to see Seiji, but he said no.

Too busy.

Two words, and he hung up.

Time passes quickly in Tokyo. After the Culture Festival at
school, Momo had two days' vacation. Would you like to go out
for dinner? I asked her, but she shook her head. I don't want to.
I have stuff to do.

Stuff to do, she said, but most of the time she stayed in her
room. She went out for a while during the day and came back
with a small bag. A book or a CD, I suppose, some such thing. I
watched, without asking, as she went to her room.

Tell me, who was it, the person you were with that day, by
the river?

A few times I almost asked, but gradually the memory has faded.

Momo has not been back to the library since that day. She
stays in her room, faint signs of her presence emanating through
her door.

A brown-eared bulbul alights on the persimmon tree. Its call is shrill. Another bulbul comes to join it. The second lands on a branch diagonal to the first, sits for a moment, then drops to a lower branch; soon, the first bird hops down as well, to another branch diagonal to the second bird. They begin flitting up and down, side to side, chirping to one another. Then a third bird comes, and I can no longer tell which bird is where, which bird chirps.

The light is new. Because it is morning. As yet unaged, fresh. I smell something cooking, and I remember the dried sardines that I am boiling. I hurry back inside, lower the flame. The fish float to the surface. And with them, small bubbles.

I turn off the stove, scoop the sardines with a wire ladle. A breeze blows in; a piece of paper, fixed with a magnet to the refrigerator, flutters. I have left the kitchen door open.

The paper rustles, flapping as though it might break free of the magnet, but it stays. Several bulbuls begin chirping, and the breeze blows.

MOMO'S HEAD IS lowered, light shines in the fine hairs on her neck.

She hates it when I touch her, so I merely look.

"I won't need a lunchbox tomorrow, Grandma. I've got cooking class."

Momo does not speak to me, only to Mother. She tries not to face me, either.

"Was I that way?" I ask mother.

"No, Kei, you weren't so even."

Even? I ask.

"That's right. You'd be stubborn one moment, then suddenly relax. One moment you were a child, and then, the very next moment, you were an adult."

"It's that age, I guess?"

That age. It's easier, I guess, to brush it aside, if you put it that way, my mother said hesitantly, squinting slightly, feeling her way. It's not that age, it's just, well, the beginning, I think.

"The beginning?"

The beginning of the end, maybe.

"The end."

Yes. That little Kei isn't here anymore, she's someone else now, that kind of end.

"Come on, I don't think it was a big event like that, was it?" I say, laughing. Mother laughs, too. It's true, people don't mature so easily. They can't. It's true, though, I suppose, even now, I'm not that consistent. We talk, back and forth, still laughing.

You want to touch Momo more, don't you? Mother says quietly.

But it's not so easy, is it, to get someone to let you touch them, she adds.

I don't know what she means, yet it startles me. I look Mother in the eye. Her expression is ordinary. Even your own child? Flesh and blood, carried in your womb? I ask, quickly.

My goodness, Kei, now you're the one being childish. Once again, Mother laughs. Whatever has come over you? You were the same way with me, you know, back then.

There is a tension in the softness of her voice. She, too, has been hurt, by me.

Do you want to try some sardines? I boiled them with *konbu* in soy sauce, I thought it might be good. It won't affect your blood pressure, if it's just a taste. It'll go well with tea, I say, trying to force my way back into the ordinary. In Tokyo, we have a life. We can hide in our everyday lives. There is nothing in Manazuru.

Well, maybe I will try some, just a taste. Mother says, in her most ordinary voice, and then, together, as if this is the routine, we sit and sip our tea.

THE NIGHT IS not yet deep.

In the imperfect darkness, diluted by innumerable lights, Seiji waits.

Seiji, I cry aloud, entering, falling into his arms.

"Are you okay?" He is surprised.

I missed you.

"Not being so aloof tonight, I see."

Aloof? I'm never aloof.

Oh, you think not? Seiji says, stroking my chin with his fingertip. Tonight, my body desires Seiji. His skin, his smell, his movements, his feelings, everything, my body desires it all.

Let's get a room right now, before dinner. I say, clutching his hand. I am sweating. Even though the air is chilly. Already, the persimmons are almost fully colored. Are they ripe? I heard Momo asking Mother. Not yet. You have to watch out, too, sometimes the persimmons on that tree can be very astringent, you know. You remember, a long time ago, your friend Yukino bit into one, and right away she spat it out, just like that, Mother answered.

We walk, entangled, into a hotel, and take a room. In the elevator, I kiss him.

"What's with you today?" Seiji asks, withdrawing slightly. The elevator comes to a halt. The doors slide open; at the end of the hall there is a door with a light over it.

Come on, that's the room, down there. I walk, pressing Seiji's back. What's up with you? Seiji asks again. I want to make love. I want to do it, with you, I tell him, speaking very fast.

Ah, I see, Seiji says, and removes his jacket. He puts it carefully on a hanger, straightens the slanting shoulders. I sit down on the large bed. I'm moving too fast, the bed bounces me.

I want you, I say out loud, I want you. Each time I say it, the yearning subsides, so I continue to repeat it. But it is only the surface wanting that subsides. The unyielding core of my desire, held back, deep inside, will not be quieted.

Please, don't run away from me, I say.

I've never run away from you, Seiji tells me, quietly.

I am confusing things. It wasn't Seiji who went away, was it. Who was it, who went away? I bury my face in Seiji's chest. He caresses my hair. You're so gentle today. Yes, because I can see that you want me to be gentle, I guess.

Don't be gentle, though. Not when we do it, don't be gentle then, I say, still speaking very fast. Seiji covers my lips with his. His large tongue enters my mouth. It is moist, it has a nice smell.

He sucks my tongue, very strong.

WE DID IT, and it was deep, but it was not enough.

And yet, even so, I was tired. We left the hotel hand in hand, our expressions mild.

"I feel like eating meat," Seiji says.

"Yes. Some animal that used to run around, in the fields, or in the mountains."

Not hard to figure out, tonight, are we? Seiji says, smiling.

The wildness lingers in my body, even in the restaurant, as we order. First, I had the waiter pour me a tall glass of mineral water, and gulped it down. Now there was a path for the water to follow within me; I felt a little better.

"Are you okay?" Seiji asked.

I don't know, I told him.

"Why are you so on edge?"

I seem on edge?

"Aren't you?"

I raise forkfuls, wordlessly, from the plate to my mouth. When there is a bone, I suck on it. Water brims in a silver bowl, and I rinse my finger in it. I dab them on the napkin, patches spread, wetting the fabric. Pushing the blade of the knife into a piece of meat, I slice down, sharply. It makes no sound, and yet it clamors.

"Are you tasting it?"

Yes, I tell him, my heart clamoring.

Seiji sighs. He peers straight into my eyes. I look down, maneuvering my knife and fork. I feel sauce at the edge of my mouth. I wipe it off with my napkin. It is hot, where I wiped.

Don't stare at me.

"Tell me, what is it, what are you scared of?" Seiji goes on staring. He ignores my entreaty. The tang of blood fills my mouth.

"Why are you scared, when I'm here with you?" His tone is calm. The clamor recedes. But a moment later, it is back.

I was remembering. I tell him, in my heart, without saying the words. I was remembering. In Manazuru. On the beach.

Seiji extends his hand, traces the bit of sauce still left at the corner of my mouth.

WHEN I GOT home, Momo was there.

She was turning the page on the calendar. It was a monthly calendar, only two months left, the pages before November torn off.

"Are you planning something?"

"No," Momo replied, brusquely.

She quickly looked away, then, changing her mind, looked back.

"How old would Dad be now, if he were alive?"

Ah, I gasp. I can't tell if it is the words, *if he were alive*, that made me gasp, or her asking, *How old would Dad be now?* Forty-seven, I guess, I answer simply, he's two years older than me.

"Dad was born in the fall?"

Was he? It's not fall, anymore, is it, in November? It had never even occurred to me, what season Rei was born in. Does she always think about these things? About her father, absent?

"I was born in spring."

That's right. You were a spring baby. Hey, would you like some cake? I change the topic. We hardly ever eat pastries together anymore. Lately, she just turns away.

"Cake! Yeah, great!" she says happily. I take plates down from the cabinet, saying nothing, careful not to disturb her cheerful mood. Cautiously I raise the box's lid, revealing the gorgeously decorated cakes.

Momo takes the cake with the chestnut on top that Seiji chose. Girls tend to like this kind of thing, don't they? he said, speaking softly, when the desserts arrived, and asked the waiter to place it, especially for Momo, in a box.

"This is good. Where's it from?" Momo asked, mashing the fine lines of whipped cream.

A place in Ebisu. It was a working dinner. I have not spoken Seiji's name to Momo. *Work*, is the word I use to simplify, to gloss over, just about everything.

"Who did you go with?"

Momo knows, by now, of my simplifications. She is poised to extract the ambiguities, the subtleties, that lie concealed within that word: work. Because she has not yet learned that even if she were to uncover the details, in the end, she would not care.

With a man.

"Someone like Dad?"

No.

It is scattering. Not like a spray of sparks, nothing so dramatic, but like a blink, an incision, the sense of hatred she feels, scattering.

How much do you remember, Momo, about Dad? I ask, ignoring her question.

"I was only three. You know that. I don't remember anything."

It's true. When Rei disappeared, Momo was only three. She has no idea where to channel what she feels. I feel pity for her. It has been a long time since I felt this way. Pity. Her mouth, full of whipped cream, her cheeks, firmer now than before, and her wrist as she brushes a loose hair from her face in irritation, all these things fill me with pity.

A step creaks. Mother must be coming down. Would you like some cake? I call brightly. Once again, Momo radiates hatred. No, I don't think so. Mother replies listlessly, on the other side of the wall.

A LETTER CAME from Rei's father.

"I have decided that my son is dead. I have settled on a posthumous name for the memorial service, and I have had a mortuary tablet prepared. Please accept my apologies for not consulting with you beforehand. No doubt I will be joining my son in the next world before long. Have you had yourself removed from the family register yet? Please feel free to arrange matters in whatever way seems best. Take care of yourself."

I recalled the house, midway up the hill in that town near the Inland Sea. The houses there were built touching adjacent houses. The town was like a maze, linked only by alleyways, perched on a steep slope. As evening descended, the smells of cooking drifted up the hill. They did not drift very far. The noises of people readying dinner in the next house down, one step down the slope, drifted up as well.

Thirteen years have passed since he disappeared.

Perhaps at last the tide is turning. All at once, all of us are accepting Rei's death.

"He got a mortuary tablet," I tell my mother.

"What's his posthumous name?"

"That wasn't in the letter."

Rei and I walked in an alley filled with cats. With every step we took, white and black and striped cats scurried across our path from gardens and gutters.

"They're like wind-up toys," I said, and Rei laughed.

We were on our way to Rei's house, to tell his parents that we were engaged to be married. It's just how it goes, you know, my parents and my sister, they were all raised here, they never left, Rei told me. It's all they know, this little town near the ocean.

They served us fish from the Inland Sea. Sashimi, grilled fish, boiled fish. It was more tender and milder than the fish in Tokyo. The soy sauce, too, was different, thicker, sweeter. I sat too long on the floor in a formal posture, my feet tucked under my rear, and my legs went to sleep. Unobtrusively, I slid them to one side.

Two years after we visited, Rei's younger sister married a man from the next town. She wore a white kimono with a hood, in the traditional style. An old man sang a wedding song. Rei and I attended the ceremony, leaving the newly born Momo with Mother. In the short time before Rei's disappearance, his sister bore her first son, Rei's mother died soon after, and the next year his sister had her second son. It seemed a very busy period, and yet it all happened in only four or five years.

"I wonder if he really died. Rei."

Mother did not answer. You're getting more white hair, aren't you? she said instead. How the everyday helps us, with its concealments. Covering up what we don't want exposed.

How would you like to write a novel? Seiji asked.

I guess I've written stories, sort of. But I'm not good with fiction.

We sat, facing each other, in a café. How many years has it been, I wonder, since Seiji and I talked about work? Not since my first essay collection, so almost a decade.

"What gave you the idea of working again with me?"

You're avoiding me, I think. There may be people who like to mix work and sex, but I am not one of them. Seiji was never that way, either.

"No particular reason," he said, and then continued, "It's just . . ."

"It's just what?"

"That I've always loved your prose, Ms. Yanagimoto."

Love. The word pains me, disgusts me.

"But why now?"

"I've always been interested in the possibility."

Don't talk to me like I'm a stranger. I almost speak the words. But Seiji has always been that way. He never laughs aloud, he speaks politely, in ten years these things have not changed.

"It's all over, then, between us?"

I sound like a desperate woman. I am, in reality, a desperate woman.

"No, that's not it," Seiji replies, quietly.

"I'm not thinking of Rei, I don't think of him at all," I say, like a tiny scream.

"I wonder about that."

It scatters. The way it did with Momo. Not like a spray of sparks, but like a fist hurling small, sharp fragments, Seiji's emotions scatter, and spread.

"Didn't you say, before, that you were jealous?"

"Jealous may not be the right word."

Then what is? I ask. Seiji's emotions scatter, keep scattering, they do not subside.

"Maybe, it's just that I have no hope."

Hope? Pain seizes the pit of my stomach. The word *love* and the word *hope* give me the same pain.

Please, let's go. It's hot in here. Let's go out, walk on a windy street, I say, clinging to him, verbally. Seiji looks down, opens his appointment book. There is beauty in his stony profile.

SEIJI, I SAY his name, twining my arms around him.

I can't take it, I say, leaning my face against his chest. I can't take it, if you go away from me.

"I've never once tried to leave you," Seiji says, hailing a cab. The words *to leave you* are engulfed by the sound of the taxi pulling up.

Tokyo Station, Seiji says.

No, not the station, someplace warm, I whisper in his ear.

"I thought you said you were hot."

I look at Seiji's face, stunned. He glares right back. He is deathly pale. How could you say something like that, a slap in the face? I ask, peering into his eyes. Without saying it.

Because I've given up, he answers, with his eyes. You'll never forget your husband.

It was obvious, this is what his fixed gaze was saying. Suddenly the taxi screeched to a halt, I fell over, onto Seiji. I hurriedly righted myself. Anger welled up at the slap he had given me. What right did he have, with no warning, to lash out like that? All of a sudden, like an animal bristling at another animal's attack, inside me, the rage is strong.

But almost immediately, it withers.

Seiji, I say, aloud. Seiji, don't go away.

"You're a terrible person," Seiji says, his voice low.

Why? I ask, trembling from the exhaustion that follows rage.

"You don't believe in anything."

The deep red bricks of Tokyo Station were dull, settled in the fading light.

Seiji. I speak his name again, just to see what will happen. He plucks change from his wallet, has the driver write him a receipt, then calmly gets out of the car.

I can't take it, I murmur. Seiji walks off toward the station, his back to me. Um, excuse me, the driver says. Excuse me, what do you want to do?

A huge truck drives by, rumbling. Cold air brushes lightly under my raised collar. Seiji keeps moving away. I can't take it, I murmur, once again.

I NOTICED THAT I was pulling the petals from a flower.

I had climbed out of the taxi, dashed across the road. There was a navy blue car, honking. The driver glared at me with twisted lips.

The second our eyes met, the tension faded from his face, quietly, it lost all expression.

Everything looks so sharp. I thought. Each minute motion of the man's face, I noted them all. He drove off, gripping the wheel. The encounter lasted only a moment, but it felt like a very long time.

I found myself standing in front of a florist. I walked in, bought some white flowers. A bouquet of a flower I didn't recognize, fewer petals than chrysanthemums but more dense than gerberas. I took them to the register, paid with a thousand-yen note, had the flowers wrapped.

I remember putting the change into my wallet.

Then, in a flash, time had passed, and I was sitting on a bench. One bench plunked down among a cluster of skyscrapers, surrounded by tall, overgrown trees that cast thick shadows, blacker even than the black of night.

Now that the sun has set, there is no one around. During the day, secretaries no doubt sat here eating their lunches, chatting, but now it is quiet, there is not even a breeze.

It feels good, watching white petals drop, in the darkness. Slowly, they flutter to the ground. I pluck one, then another.

There are so many flowers on each stem, my fingers never rest.

A small white heap forms on the earth at my feet. The poor things, don't you feel sorry for them? I remember the sound of my voice, chastising Momo, when she was two. Poor Mr. Flower, it hurts, it hurts him very much, you know, when you do that. Momo had pulled up a yellow flower blooming in a field, she was pulling out its petals, lost in it, and I had said those words to her.

Mr. White Flower, it hurts, it hurts, Mr. Yellow Flower, it hurts, I say to myself, with my voice, in my head.

It's nauseating. This made-up voice of mine. And the words I'm speaking.

A flower's pain, what do I know? I've never known it. How could I tell Momo such a thing? And yet, she stopped. Puwa flower, huwt, huwt, Mommy? She said, beaming up at me.

We got up, left the field behind. Momo tossed away the flower. I pretended I hadn't seen, and we went back home, having fun together, holding hands.

WHEN I GOT home, Momo and Mother both looked utterly ordinary.

"I'm home," I said, and they both greeted me, hello. The second I stepped into the living room, something was wrong.

There, on the wall, in a white, open space, stuck there.

"Rei!" I blurted out.

Old photographs, a number of them, were pinned up.

"I was going through some old things, and I found them. There were lots," Mother said, turning away, just a little.

"I put them up," Momo said, covering Mother's words with her own.

Not all were photographs of Rei. Me, holding a tiny, tiny Momo, in her first month. Rei's parents, beaming, posing before a low table lined with half-empty cups. A picture of Rei's sister's children, the two boys, tangled up, laughing. She sent it, I believe, when the older boy was five, when they took him to the shrine, on November 15th, for the festival that day. Already, by then, Rei had disappeared.

Intentionally, I suppose, the pictures' edges have been made to overlap, a bit, they are hung at a slight angle, arranged attractively.

There is one of me with my parents. I remember, clearly, when it was taken. It was spring vacation, before I entered eleventh grade, Father had just come back from the town where he lived, where his company had relocated him. We were going to have dinner at a restaurant in Ginza, all dressed up, we took the picture in the garden. There was a nip in the air that evening, my father perched the camera on the gate, set it so the shutter would go off by itself. It didn't work the first time. The second time, Mother set the timer. You know, I just realized, it's bad luck to take a picture with three people, isn't it? Kei, get a small doll, or that figurine in the entryway, maybe, the glass one, bring that out, will you? You can keep it hidden in your hand, as long as it's in the picture.

I ran inside, grabbed the glass figurine. I felt its coolness in my hand. My heart pounded when the photos were developed, a shot of the three of us, but with another, invisible. Three, and yet four. Only, three.

A dozen or so old pictures, that one among them, on the wall.

"We'd put them away, I guess," I said, and Momo stared, unmoving.

"When you put them up and look like this, it seems so real."

So real. Momo enunciated the words, those two, very clearly.

"Well, it was real," I said, and Momo cocked her head.

"I know, but for me, I don't remember it, whether it's real, or not."

Mother laughs loudly.

Rei's eyes, in the photograph, stare fixedly at something. I don't remember what.

I WONDER IF Seiji will agree to meet me.

Agree, not agree, I am startled to find myself using these words. Did he agree to meet me? And did he, sometimes, not agree? Was it like that, the way we were?

I can't take it, I shake my head.

Pushing all that from my mind, I call Seiji. I hate calling. I told Seiji this once, a while ago. I don't like it that, when I call, I can't see you, can't see how you are.

I'm fine, however I am, Seiji replied.

I laughed at the word, fine. It was true, he seemed fine. Always calm, quiet, never shaken.

"Can we—" I begin, but his voice, steely, interrupts.

"This is a bad time."

"But—" I say, strong.

"I mean it, I can't now."

It is true, I can't see how he is. I listen for sounds in the background, but I hear nothing. Is he outside, or in a room? He picked up the phone so he probably isn't in a meeting, maybe he stepped out to answer, but if he has decided not to answer my calls, he wouldn't have stepped out.

I hate it, calling.

I think again. It doesn't have to be now, when you're free, call me, I say, and Seiji hesitates, there is something he cannot make up his mind to say.

Please, don't call me again.

He is about to say this, but he hesitates, is that it?

What has made Seiji this way, it makes no sense.

You don't believe in anything.

I don't understand, those words that he said. Because I do believe. How could I have had a child, if I didn't believe, it's impossible. And I couldn't have gone on seeing him, either, without believing. I couldn't keep breathing, to keep myself alive, if I didn't believe.

And yet, I had a feeling, faint, very faint, that perhaps I knew I didn't.

I don't believe in anything.

Since that day? The day Rei disappeared?

Calmly, quietly, with a sense of finality, Seiji hung up. He's fine, even without me, I think. The welling tears blur my vision slightly.

You're a fool, the woman says.

It has been a while since she has come, and followed.

It's not Rei I'm worried about now, I say coldly, and the woman leers.

My, my, how busy the living are, she says, chuckling.

It is true, all my life, I've been busy, changing. I see one landscape in the morning, and by noon it has changed. I feel one way at night, and in the morning things are different. Last year's hats are out of fashion now, I don't wear them anymore.

"Momo and I, we're different now, too." I tell the woman, plaintively, without thinking. Though I know enough not to expect sympathy.

"It's true, it's like that, especially with children."

Unexpectedly, she responds.

"You watch them so closely, enjoying, rejoicing at how they change, until one day, all of a sudden, just like that, off they go."

I see Momo's face. Turned away. The curve from the base of her ear to her chin is so gentle, and yet the sense of determination I see there is hard.

Yesterday, my heart was pounding over Rei, today it pounds over Seiji. Yesterday, I would gather Momo in my arms, hold her, today she has escaped me, and I stand watching her leave, numb.

"Really, always so caught up in things, I feel like a fool."

We're all the same. Seiji, was that his name? From over here, he's no different, just another fool. What point is there in refusing you like that, so stubbornly? the woman says.

Pain stabs the pit of my stomach. *Refusing* is the word that hurts.

Isn't there anything constant? I ask the woman, wondering what she will say. She turns her head ambiguously. Is she telling me yes, or no? Or is it, perhaps, neither one?

Why not throw it away, into the ocean, she says, after a while.

It feels good. Hurling it, sending it flying, into the distance.

I recall the figure of the woman, whenever it was, throwing her twins away, into the water. The waves were rough. She hugged the child to her chest, tenderly, before she threw it in. Her arm was supple and strong, she betrayed no hesitation at all. She threw the twins, one at a time, away. The two babies soon swallowed up, under the tall waves.

FOR A MONTH, two months, I did not hear from Seiji.

Another year began.

"I'm a year older, by the old way of counting," Mother says. "Next year, I'll be seventy."

You get two years older, every year, the old way? Momo asks, puzzled. No, in the old way of counting, you would add a year to the ones you already have at the beginning of each new year, that's how it worked, Mother tells her. I still don't understand, Momo laughs. Why did people back in olden times want to count like that when it made them older?

"Is that what I am? A person from olden times?" Mother laughs, too.

I guess, back then, people thought it was a wonderful thing to live long, so they wanted to get older and older, don't you think? Mother says. Mmm. Momo nods agreeably.

It strikes me as funny, this weirdly unremarkable conversation taking place at the same time that I am so caught up in thoughts of Seiji, and I smile.

Picking at the New Year's dishes Mother and I have made, half her, half me, I prepare the main dish, a soup with *mochi*. We never have sea bream or shrimp for New Year's in our house, Momo says, dissatisfied. Sea bream and shrimp, those are just symbolic, you know, they don't actually taste that good, Mother tells her. I don't see how that can be true, there is always shrimp in the prepared New Year's meals they sell, sometimes a whole sea bream, too.

I recalled the New Year's soup at Rei's parents' house. The first New Year's after we married, on the first day of the new year, I prepared the soup the way they made it there. On the second day, I made it in the Tokyo style, as my mother had taught me, with clear broth, *komatsuna* and chicken, a sprig of *mitsuba* floating on top, the *mochi* toasted.

In the region where Rei was born, the cakes of *mochi* were round, they were not toasted, the broth was made with *konbu* and flavored with white miso. Daikon and carrots gave it color. I enjoyed it more, because I was unaccustomed to the flavor.

"Ah, the air is always so clear on New Year's day," Rei said, stretching out on the tatami. He had been drinking spiced New Year's sake, then regular sake, too, his face was flushed. You really get drunk when you drink during the day, he said, and a second later he was snoring.

I wonder if Seiji is with his family now, too.

I think, curious how it will feel, and the pit of my stomach aches. I have never been jealous of Seiji's wife or his children.

Because it is unclear to me what family means. I did not create the family into which I was born. The family I tried to create broke, so easily. I have never, really, sensed it, what a family is.

I am jealous now.

Not of their being family, but because they have a reason to be close with Seiji.

In the lacquer boxes of New Year's food, there are now gaps where the food has been eaten, revealing the bottom of the box, sticky, gleaming. Once I have filled the gaps with more food, I will forget that the gaps were ever there.

I felt an unpleasant sensation. Once more, the pit of my stomach ached.

IT IS HERE, but it isn't.

I open my laptop, type the words.

A novel, Seiji said. I have not heard from him, even now, when the New Year's decorations that stood outside the front door, pine and bamboo, are gone. I recall, from a distance, a woman planting bulbs, in a scene in a story that I wrote a while ago. The woman buries several crocus bulbs in a corner of the garden, but before they grow, before the flowers bloom, she leaves.

Was it because of Rei, that I wrote about a woman who leaves home? The story was based on the things Rei had done, yet without realizing it I made the woman do them.

"She isn't happy, in the end," Seiji said, after reading it. He was not involved with the story, it was for another publisher, so this wasn't until after it was published. I had not told him about it. But he found it after some time, and he had read it, without telling me.

"Who?" I asked, not understanding.

"The woman, who left."

I had not written about what happened to her after she left. I wrote only about the man left behind, staring blankly at the deep yellow bed of crocuses, pouring myself into the writing.

"I didn't sense any happiness rising up from the prose."

I should hope not, going off like that, it wouldn't be fair for her to be happy suddenly, I told him, I think. Seiji smiled faintly. Then, ever so slightly, his face darkened.

It isn't here, and yet it is.

I flip the words, type them on the second line.

I can't write a novel. I am too distracted by the affairs of this world, I lack the self-possession to enter into the act of imagining what is not here. Rei, who isn't here, but is; and Seiji, who is here, yet isn't. It is maddening. Maddening, and, sad, I yearn to be with him.

It startles me, how attached I am to Seiji. But he is here, so I cling. If he left, I would have nothing to hold on to.

Why not throw it away, into the ocean.

I remember the woman's words.

Perhaps I will throw it away.

I HEARD SEIJI'S voice.

Not because he called. I went to the office of a different publisher, not his, to discuss a project. After the meeting, as soon as I got in the elevator, I heard his voice.

"We'll have to celebrate!" the voice said.

Looking up, I saw a broad-shouldered man with clear skin, nothing like Seiji.

"Is something wrong?" the man said.

By the time we reached the ground floor, everyone but the man and I had exited the elevator. I had been staring straight at him.

"Your voice," I whispered.

My voice? he asked, peering at me.

"Your voice, it sounds just like someone I know."

What kind of person is he, that man?

"Someone whose voice I yearn to hear, but can't."

Without meaning to, I had told him the truth. It wasn't the sameness of his voice, it was the way he was standing, that made me say it.

"Well, then, I'm happy to let you hear it," the man said, and put his hand around my waist. It was an unnatural movement, but he made it natural. We went, together, to a hotel.

I sweated a lot.

I didn't think I could do it with anyone but Seiji, it had been so long.

But I could. It was easy.

With Seiji, and Rei, too, it was easy.

To grow distant. To go where I could not see them.

"You're beautiful," the man told me.

"It was because I wanted it," I replied.

"I'd like to do this again."

"We can, but I doubt it will be better than today," I said, honestly.

That's all right. That's how it is, usually. A lot of the time, the way things actually are, and the way they feel, aren't the same. No one remembers how they really were, you know, not really, he said, his expression serious.

I don't remember it, whether it's real, or not.

I recall Momo's words.

They seem similar to the man's, but different. They were different, and yet it struck me that in the end, perhaps it was the same thing, after all.

Great, let's get together again, then, I said, manufacturing a smile. Knowing, even as I spoke, that there would be no second time.

I washed the sweat away in the shower, but the smell lingered, faintly, on my shoulders.

I PULLED MY right pajama leg free and took a few steps, the left still on.

A morning bath. I would run the washing machine while I soaked. Losing myself in housework let me forget Seiji, so lately I hardly ever left the house. The air inside was humid and warm. I would forget it all, everything.

My cell phone launched into its delirious music.

This early? I thought, wary, and went out, one pajama leg on, the other trailing on the floor.

It was Seiji.

Oh, good morning!

My tone was bright. What am I supposed to say, in this state, with one leg in my pajamas, making excuses for myself, to myself, but I can't explain this to Seiji.

"I'm afraid it's been quite a while since I called. How've you been?"

Very polite speech, more intimate speech, mixed. As always.

What is it? Has something happened? I ask, growing worried. He wasn't the sort of person who could go back, just like that, to the way things were before, acting as though nothing had happened. I felt concern for Seiji, first, before the anxiety of waiting, the annoyance.

"No, everything's fine."

A warm sweat, something like that, spreads across my body.

"It makes me happy to hear your voice."

Before I can think, I am speaking the words. Seiji falls silent. I have been rebuffed.

"How is the novel going?"

"How is it going?" Rebuffed, his call still pleases me, I parrot his words.

"Are you writing?"

I'm writing, a little.

My novel, a mere two lines written. Seiji has thrown me away. I listen to his voice, and that is clear. But I am happy. Simply to hear his voice, in my ear.

Goodbye, I think, pulling my pajamas from my leg. I toss them into the washer, push the button. I measure out the detergent, sprinkle it into the machine as it begins to fill. I stroke the top of my naked thigh, to see how it will feel. It feels smooth, and soft. Read it, when I've written it, I tell Seiji, and hang up. What did Seiji want to tell me, I wonder? So early in the morning.

The washing machine goes round, making a whirlpool. Some detergent remains, undissolved by the cold water this winter morning. The water spirals, splashing up.

I rest my hand against the door to the bathroom, I recall the softness of Seiji's lips. They felt like thick petals. Seiji, I say, just to see how it feels. No one answers. No one is there. Everyone retreats from me, goes away.

seven

M Y BODY IS pulled, almost dragged.
It is not, exactly, that I want to go, it is simply that I go.

"Manazuru, again?" Mother asked, as I was leaving.

I remember Momo, slipping on her shoes in the entryway, calling out to Mother, I'm going. With my chopsticks I lifted a bite from the heap of bacon and eggs on my plate and hurriedly shoved it into my mouth. I remember, too, feeling it catch, a strangled pressure at the base of my throat, as I swallowed. Had I fixed the bacon and eggs, or was it Mother, that is something I do not remember. I do not remember, either, taking my plate into the kitchen and washing it. I went straight to my room, took a heavy sweater from the chest of drawers, donned my coat and scarf, put my wallet and a pair of underwear, nothing else, in a small bag, stepped over the brown slippers that Momo had not bothered to straighten in the front hall, grasped the door handle. It was then that Mother spoke.

"That's right."

"What is it, in Manazuru?" Mother asked, pain in her expression.

I look away.

Long ago, when Father was still alive, I dreamed of Mother making love. The smooth skin of her back, pale against the surrounding duskiness, was all I saw, I could not see her face, and yet I knew, dreaming, that it was Mother. Was the man she was with Father, or not? I was not interested. Mother, making love, was all that mattered.

I was scared. And also, relieved. I didn't want to see, but now, at last, I had seen, I did not have to prepare myself for what I might see, and I felt deeply relieved.

I saw the same pain in Mother's back, in my dream, that I read in her face.

"There isn't anything, I'm just going."

A voice, unlike mine, replied, and yet it was my voice, and I left.

THE TRAIN TO Tokyo Station was packed.

My body tilted as the train pulled out, I could not move between stations. I had become a branch, and when I looked around we were all the same, a branch, a clinging vine, some parasitic plant, all in a tangle, chaos.

At each station, it was like a breath: a human exhalation, and then the sucking in. It was mesmerizing agony. Mesmerizing, perhaps, because I was empty. I could never accept this rapture when my body brimmed with business, so many plans to be made, people to meet, like tight rows of insect eggs planted there.

I got off at Tokyo Station, boarded an outbound train. I sat on the ocean side. I could not yet see the ocean, but I could smell it.

"Looks like rain," a woman, diagonally across, said to the man with her.

Outside, the sky was faintly colored. Not gray, not blue, either, it was a pale color, like when you squeeze a brand new watercolor from its tube, and a tiny bead of colored water, a diluted red, if it's red, a diluted black, if it's black, trickles out, slowly, around the rim of the thick, viscous blob of paint, the sky was pale like that.

The smell was rain, then, not the ocean. It started falling soon after Fujisawa, pricking the ocean's surface, which had been passing in and out of view since Ninomiya.

I recall the pain on Mother's face, as I was leaving.

And Seiji's, too.

The first time I visited Manazuru, the season was, just a little, closer to spring. Kites were flying. The sky went on so far you couldn't tell how far it went.

"We'll have to buy umbrellas somewhere, I guess," the woman says.

"We'll be okay, once we're in the car," the man replies.

The couple's fingertips, lightly intertwined, are too clear to me. Her nails are painted red, his ring finger has a hangnail, she has a tiny mole on her pinky, a callus at his second joint, all of it appears to me with such clarity, it is like looking into a microscope.

"You won't die, will you?" the woman says.

Have I misheard? I do not listen more closely.

The man makes no response.

"Don't die, please?" she says, once again.

I did not mishear. But I do not have the energy.

Soon we are at Manazuru. Her thin fingers toy restlessly with his.

IT IS A fierce rain.

I buy a clear plastic umbrella at the kiosk, hurry out onto the street. There is no bus to the shore for an hour. I will go on foot, I decide, hug my bag tightly to me.

Mud splashes up my legs. I'm back, I call, to the woman who always comes and follows, in Manazuru.

There is no answer.

After twenty minutes' walking, I begin to grow numb. I peer up through the clear umbrella. The plastic is clouded by the spattering rain, I can't make out anything at all. The bottom of my coat, soaked, clings to my legs.

Where the road begins to drop, there is a cluster of stores. A soba shop with its name on a tall, narrow banner, is open. It is lunchtime, it is packed. I order *nabeyaki* udon.

Sipping the soup, I burn my tongue. As I eat, slowly, the crowd thins out. There's a guesthouse near here, isn't there, run by some people named Suna? I ask the young woman serving me. For no real reason. Oh, the place near the shore, Minatoya, you mean?

Something like a woman's shadow comes.

I scoop up the last bit of soup in my spoon, gulp it down. The shadow crouches, wavering, by my waist. You always come where there is food, I mumble, and it tightens, just a little.

When I leave the restaurant, the rain has stopped. The sky is darker than when it was raining. Treading carefully on the gray road, I head for the shore.

THE WAVES ARE high.

I try to think of Seiji, but I can't.

When you come to Manazuru, give yourself to Manazuru. It is the woman's voice.

She was a shadow, but now, suddenly, she has a form, perfectly visible. She has long hair, she is even more lovely than before, and her voice is clear.

"Did you get a room?" the woman asks.

"No, I don't know if I'll stay here tonight."

"You'd better, or you might not be able to get back."

What do you mean by that? I ask, but she won't say.

I walk out onto the beach with her. We're like friends, the two of us, I say, and she smiles. She offers me her hand, and I take it, firmly, in mine.

"It's the first time. The first time we've been this way, so together," she says, very quietly.

We sit on a damp rock, gaze out into the offing. There is a long bridge that spans the bay. We are still holding hands. I feel her warmth, it is like a living hand.

"Why?" I ask, and the woman tilts her head.

"I'm not sure, maybe it's that we're closer, now, than we were," she replies.

She is so very close, now, is that what drew me back to Manazuru?

"I want to see Rei," I say, earnest, just to see.

"Do you really?"

"I do."

"If you can't go back?"

"I won't go back."

"And your daughter?"

"My daughter has gone, too."

Has she, really? The woman frowns. It's not so easy, you know.

"It doesn't have to be easy," I say, lingering over each word. I squeeze the woman's hand, strongly. It crumbles. Where her hand was, there is only empty space. She herself is gone.

Don't go. I call to her.

The waves are high. Two black trucks speed by, rumbling, one after the other, over the bridge. The woman does not return.

DID IT ALWAYS feel this way, such a lack, of presence?

I have been wandering now, for a long time. From the beach, I climbed a slightly steep hill, prayed at a shrine to Sarasvatī. A few statues shone dimly in the dark wooden building. There is something in these remote areas, in the place where a god lives, even in the midst of decay, that soothes. You feel that you are in a place you recognize.

I huddled for a while, wondering if something familiar would come, but nothing did.

I grew cold, and walked on. I descended the stairway, skirted an isolated cluster of houses, gazed at the trees in their neat, well-kept gardens. The windows of all the houses were shuttered. There is no feeling of presence here, at all. I climbed the steps, putting all my weight on them, slowly, one at a time, to Chigo Shrine. Here, too, no sense of presence, either within the shrine itself, or in the space around it.

I returned to a path that led off to the side, partway up. The way was narrow, lined on both sides by houses. Every gate was shut. Satsuma oranges, tiny fruit, hung heavy from the trees. A bird came, and cried. Only the bird's raucous cry breaks the silence.

It is hard, climbing, descending. I see an elementary school and listen for children's voices, but here, too, I do not feel a presence. Wind gusts across the puddles in the playground, raising tiny waves. A bell sounds. I wait, wondering if someone might come out of the school. But no figure appears. The classrooms are all dark, settled in their stillness.

Hey, I call, to no one in particular.

Hey. Once again.

I walk faster, pass stone figures of the two Dōsojin, guardians of travelers, arrive at the fire station. Red fire trucks are parked in a row, looking cold, not moving here, either. I decide to leave the back streets, go down to the road that the bus takes.

I do not see a single car, no matter how far I walk. No buses pass. At a stop, I check the schedule. The next bus is in ten minutes. During the festival, in the summer, it was around here that the boat capsized. I am cold, I look around for a store to enter, but all are closed.

Sitting down on the bench, I realize how thirsty I am, and I go to buy a can of coffee from the vending machine. I never drink sweet coffee, but that is what I select. I return to the bench, wrap my hands around the can, and wait. It was hot, but soon it cools.

I pull the tab, and drink. I look at the bus schedule, again, and check my watch. The next bus is in ten minutes. After I finish my coffee, I check my watch again. Ten minutes until the bus.

Alone, a kite flies. Tracing small circles, it stays near the water.

TEN MINUTES UNTIL the bus.

How many times have I checked?

What sort of place have I wandered into?

The wind blows, weakly. A few seagulls perch on the booth where tickets are sold for the boat tour around the peninsula. Grass grows on the sagging roof. The seagulls' cries are shrill.

The fish market, the cluster of ramen shops and bars at the edge of the market, the quarry on the mountainside, everything, I realize, is crumbling, decaying. The blacktop is laced with a web of cracks, and here, too, thin stalks of grass have grown, in clumps.

A swarm of mosquitoes rises in a column over the bench at the bus stop. It is winter, and yet the bugs buzz about, thickly.

Come back.

It is the woman's voice.

But I cannot tell where she is. Ten minutes until the bus. I am petrified, afraid to leave the bus stop. I am thinking of Rei, like a ringing in my ears. I loved him. The truth, though, is, even now, I do not know the meaning of that word. *Love.* Maybe, I should just accept that the feeling I had within me, then, when I thought of Rei, was loving. Useless as it is, this loving. Especially in a place like this. Still, I loved Rei. I think about this, now.

Even after he went away, I loved him. I could not cease loving him. It is hard to love what is not there. The feeling of loving, somehow, insinuates itself into your love. Like a bag turned inside-out, the feeling is turned on itself.

Does love, reversed, become the opposite of love?

It doesn't.

Is love's opposite hatred? Or is hatred a synonym of love? It was never neat, either way. It was never so easy.

It became indistinct, stagnant, obscure, different.

Ten minutes until the bus.

It is cold. The kite keeps flying, around and around, in one place.

I WALKED WITH Rei through a field, one spring.

Holding Momo, walking, in a vast field of yellow forsythia and white snow willow.

"Look, a swing," Rei said.

I passed Momo to him, got on the swing. I soared, looked down over Rei and Momo. Each time I catapulted forward and up, or back and up, Momo squealed with glee.

I relaxed my legs, let momentum carry me, and immediately the swing began to settle into smaller arcs. I thought it would stop soon, but it continued. On and on, in small arcs.

Rei sets Momo on the ground, walks around behind me. He pushes my back. Once again the swing swings widely. Momo tries to stand up. She is incapable, still, of walking by herself. For a moment she rises, stands, feet planted firmly on the ground. Then she plops down on her bottom. She opens her legs where she sits, claps her palms together, delighted.

Rei stands behind me, pushes me, strong, each time the swing returns.

That's enough, stop, I say, but Rei just laughs. Bright, strong laughter.

When I close my eyes, the arcs feel bigger. I am swinging, not over a space of two meters, forward and back, but up into the heavens, then back down to earth, is how it feels.

If I let go of these two chains, how far would I be thrown?

I think, deep in my head, not near my eyelids, but at the core.

Each time Rei's palm presses into my back, my body returns to earth, but there is something else, not my body, not my heart, either, something unknown, indistinct, that has ascended into the heavens, that will not come back.

When I opened my eyes, it was just a field, and when Momo and Rei turned to me, they had the same look in their eyes.

I threw my feet against the earth, strongly, stopping the swing. Momo kept clapping.

Scooped up, high, in Rei's arms, Momo laughed even louder.

It was autumn, in the same field.

At the edge of the field, there was a station for a gondola lift.

Over the mountain, along a low-hanging steel cable, like a beetle scrabbling over the earth, a small, angular gondola crept.

Let's take it, Rei said.

I didn't want to ride it, but we did.

There was a second station partway up, everyone disembarked but Rei and me. Only we were left in the gondola, pulled mechanically along, a recorded voice playing over the loudspeakers.

At the third station, the lift stopped. The voice fizzled, the gondola appeared to have broken down, and yet Rei sat gazing, perfectly calm, out the window.

"Maybe we can climb out and cut the gondola free from the cable," Rei suggested, with the air of one struck by inspiration.

It will never work, I said, realizing that this must be a dream. And if I'm dreaming, I think, maybe it would be all right to cut the gondola free?

We stepped out onto the windswept platform, pressed the emergency button, and slowly the gondola descended to earth. Crashing down onto the slope, the metal buckled, dug in.

"Rei, I'm scared. What are we doing here, in this place?" I ask.

"Oh, it's always like this, we're just living our lives," Rei answers.

Fierce gusts blow, let up, then come again. It seems we will be carried away. Even though it is a dream, there is nothing tentative in the chill of the wind, or its fierceness.

Far below, I can see the autumn field. I put my arm around Rei's waist. Yesterday, come to think of it, when Rei came home from work, as I was arranging his suit on its hanger, I found myself calling up the image of a gondola crushed in the earth, screws scattered, the glittering silver of twisted steel.

Yes, it's true, you live, and these things happen, all the time.

Yeah, tell me about it, all the time.

We say, to each other. The autumn wind tousles our hair. I wait, slightly annoyed, wondering what I will cook for dinner, hoping the next gondola will come soon.

THE SAME FIELD, again, but it was neither spring nor autumn, but late summer.

I was getting on his case.

About the woman. The one with the mole on her neck.

Rei said nothing. He won't even make excuses, I thought, chilled, and turned to look at him, he was staring straight ahead, no expression on his face.

My Rei had withdrawn, deep down, into the container of Rei, what stood before me now was nothing but the shape.

I slapped his cheek.

Rei blanched. But still he did not speak.

It's not her fault, he said quietly, after a time.

You don't love me now? I asked.

Love, Rei murmured, uncertain. I can't get used to words like that.

Once again, I am chilled.

I had the sense that all the words we had spoken together, Rei and I, had whirled in the air, becoming something else, taking on different meanings.

I clung to Rei.

He didn't push me back, but for just an instant, he pulled away.

I had thought we were family, the borders between our bodies indistinct, Momo and Rei and I, the three of us, mingling, dissolving.

In the field, in late summer, Rei's body repelled me.

Still, I clung. Pressed my lips to his ears, whispered, Don't go.

Lightly, he held me. We were closer, and yet he seemed to be distancing me. Though he held me, because he was holding me, I felt lonely.

I won't let you go, I screamed.

Rei held me tighter. Like a child having a tantrum.

Suddenly, fury seized me. If I had a knife, how I'd plunge it into you, I thought.

My body drenched in the blood shooting out from him, I would wait until the last drop had trickled out, make sure it was over, then strongly, strongly, clasp Rei to me, I would press my face against his body, if I could.

Rei looked at me, calmly.

I couldn't even cry. He looked at me, and my body wanted him, madly. I should not have loved, I thought. It would have been better if none of this had happened.

Rei's gaze hurt me. It hurt, and I was glad. I was so sad, so lonely, and yet I was glad.

Rei. I called his name.

Kei. He called me back.

In the field, in late summer, a column of mosquitoes whirled, thick.

Ten minutes until the bus. I sit on the bench near the shore in Manazuru, feeling numb, the mosquitoes droning.

A LARGE SHADOW passes.

As I glance up, a bird sails by. I hear its white wings slice the wind.

"A heron."

I say the word, and my body, seemingly stuck to the bench, loosens, just a little.

The heron crosses the peak, out of view. I check my watch. The short hand and the long hand have both stopped, ten minutes before the time when the bus is to come. And yet the second hand is moving.

The heron returns. It was alone, but it flies back with a second trailing behind. The first lands on the roof of a house by the mountain. The second settles on the roof of the next house over, finds a place to stand, its long legs slightly bent, and freezes.

Half the tiles have slid from the roofs. Moss has filled the gaps between those that remain, and some sort of thatch has grown up around the moss. The rain shutters, pulled halfway out along their tracks, are starting to decay.

Abandoned houses stand empty, foreboding, for a decade or so, but if they are left longer than that, they begin anew, they are reborn as living things. Vines have squeezed through the cracked glass, where the windows are not shielded by the shutters. The leaves are mostly brown and withered, but underneath, already, tiny shoots of new green are visible.

The walls are blackened, cracked. The fissures run boldly up and down, side to side, as if they were drawn there by someone, on purpose. It is not that the house is losing its form, ceasing to be what it was as it is taken over by the snaking vines, rising grasses, it is that the decaying structure itself is acquiring a new life, different from before, that is how it seems.

I stand, walk over to the houses where the herons stand.

They are facing in opposite directions. Their feathers are white. Their beaks are black. The tips of their feet, powerful, gripping the roofs, are yellow.

I rest my hand on the bug-eaten gate, and pull. A hinge pops free, and the gate screeches, falling. The garden is not so overgrown. Light, short grasses nod in the wind, that is all.

I keep going, reach the front door, I had assumed it would be locked, but when I pull on the handle, it gives, just like that, and I go inside without removing my shoes.

The odor of mold envelops me. Holding my breath, I push the frame of a *shōji* divider, the paper torn, slide it on its track. Three photographs are hung over the lintel, a woman with her hair done up, on the right, then a man in formal attire, then a small baby lying on his futon, each in a narrow frame, hung at an angle so that the person gazes down, protectively, over those who walk below.

You must have died, still a baby, I think, looking at the picture on the left.

The sparkle in his goggling eyes reminds me of Momo. In a separate, square corner of the room, in the back, a Buddhist altar sits dully. The gold leaf has tarnished over the years. Though the baby is no one I know, tears fill my eyes.

How long, I wonder, have these houses been so dark?

The nameplates are decayed, illegible. From house to house, from room to room, I walk, leaving footprints on the dusty tatami, in the halls of buildings that looked as if they were abandoned only after every trace of the lives lived there had been expunged.

The woman does not come and follow. Even though, on the beach, she had a form.

At some point, more herons came, there is one, now, on the roof of each house. Plodding through the houses, I think of the herons, beyond the ceilings, above the attics and crawl spaces, perched. The herons, unmoving, white, isolated lights in a dark, still scene.

I called, and Rei came.

"I'm lonely," I said, and Rei smiled faintly.

"Hold me."

Rei did not hold me. Instead, he peered into my eyes. His gaze had always been so strong, but when he looked at me, now, it was thin and weak.

"Do you want to come, here?" he asked.

I want to be together, I think. But what if, in order to be with you, I must give up being? It is not easy to decide. To give up being, with you. To give up being with you.

"Will you come?" he asked, again.

"I don't want it to end."

Which is it? Rei smiled, again, faintly.

"That's not the sort of thing you can decide on your own, I guess," he whispered, very low. The sound of him, whispering, is so familiar, so dear.

"How did you decide, Rei?"

You know me, Rei says, peering once more into my eyes. It is stronger than before. Light shines on his irises. I knew them, all along. These eyes. I liked to hold my face close to his, gaze into them. I tried not to forget what it was like, then, that instant, looking, or the next one, or the next after that, each moment, gazing so earnestly it was like a prayer. I held his cheeks between my palms, pleading, please, don't go away, please, be mine?

What are you talking about, we're married, right? Rei answered, baffled.

Even being together, it's not enough. Even together, it aches.

It's not enough, just being here, together? he said, slightly irritated.

It's you, your being you, that makes me this way.

You're very passionate about me, I see that, Kei, he said, laughing, pressing my face back as I moved closer. Not to be mean, very gently.

His gentleness sent me the other way, jerked me back, I felt, beyond.

The thoughts that held me. Like sinking into a lake, its depths unfathomed, down through the clear water, deeper and deeper, until, as your body mingles with the bubbles that surge up, past it, your body, too, smoothes out, becomes round, takes the form of a bubble, and finally arrives at the very bottom, where it is spherical, and does not move.

Rei knew nothing of those thoughts. But then, neither did I. Know anything of Rei's thoughts. Or of Mother's. Or Father's. Or Seiji's.

I know nothing. How far have I come, in ignorance.

I TOOK REI'S hand, and walked on.

Left the field behind, dove through the water, dissolved into the void, returned to the field, walked on, without end.

Rei came quietly, led by the hand, my hand.

It's a long way, we've come.

I'm tired.

I sit down, heavily, on a bench at the end of the field. Rei sits down beside me. I wrap my arms around his body, lean against him. He runs his hand through my hair. You've aged, he says. What do you mean, are you telling me you haven't, since then? I ask.

I couldn't say. I can't see myself.

Filled with tenderness, I squeeze him harder. Herons fly. A flock of dozens, spreading their wide wings, over the field, so smooth it is as if they are sliding on ice, flying away.

Did I kill you, Rei?

There is no answer.

I strangled him. And yet, he did not die. I'm not so frail that you could choke me, Kei, that a woman's hands could do me in. Rei was chuckling. I slapped his cheek. The quiet smack did not echo, it simply faded, uselessly. That didn't even hurt. Try again, Rei chuckled.

I wanted to kill him. For him to die, not by another's hand, but by my own.

Why, loving, do I break through, beyond? I thought I had a true sense of the weight of his body, but then, somewhere along the way, his body lost its form, it was clear, the hand I stretched out passed, helplessly, through, beyond, a place that had been body before.

As Rei sits beside me on the bench, I probe his body. From his hips to his ribs, from his chest to his neck, along his chin to his mouth nose forehead, I am unable to hold back, I kiss him, saliva dribbles down, I devour him, wrap my arms, strongly, around his back, squeeze him, speak his name, I miss him, even sitting here, next to him, no gap between us, my missing him does not thin, I am sad, I feel sad, I feel as if my body will vanish, utterly vanish, leaving only the feelings, the feelings scatter, there will be nothing there, and even then this missing him will not be extinguished, there is no end, the herons, they are flying away.

I pulled my body back, stared at Rei, intently.

A man with jet black hair, breathing, warm, indifferent.

Oh, darling, our baby, who was so little, she has grown up now, so big. She's moved away from me, she's headed somewhere else, alone. Her eyes, that reckless look, she has your eyes, and soon, I know, she'll begin, hating and loving, fiercely.

Rei grinned.

Mo-mo.

He spoke her name, rolled it on his tongue.

The herons descended. One, then a second, waving, to the field.

I FELT THE urge to put my arms around Rei, again, and reached for him.

The body I expected to be there, was not.

I tighten my embrace. My arms form a ring, overlap, I am holding myself.

Have you gone?

I call.

No, I'm here.

The woman comes.

It's not you, I'm calling. It's Rei.

Rei, he was never here, she says, and it seems to me that she is probably right. I check the schedule hanging at the bus stop by the bench, there are still ten minutes until the bus, there is nothing but herons flocking in the field.

"I'm so tired."

More tired, even, than before, I say plaintively to the woman. I am looking to her for help. The humor of it strikes me. I have been tired before, many, many times. So tired I want to burst out screaming, I want to break into a moan, I want to rage, that is how tired I am, and yet my heart, alone, quickens, my body cannot keep up, and so, evermore, it is quickening, I feel, in my heart, I am about to burst forth, out of myself, so weary I have felt.

But, at some point, I learned how to soothe the weariness.

"It's true, most of the time, these things can be fixed," the woman agrees.

All around the woman, people gather, the men and women she is tied to. An old woman. A young woman. An old man. A man who is not so young. A young man. A child. A second child. All her relatives, every one, coming to touch her. One holds her foot. Another her arm. One rides her shoulders. One is wrapped around her neck.

"They weigh on you, these things," the woman says, lightly shaking them off.

Most of them fall from her. But soon they come back, clinging. Some hold fast even when she shakes, refusing to leave her. There is no end to it.

"I'm used to it, though."

The child on her knee is the most tenacious. She has entwined herself around the woman's knee, tightly, squeezing with both arms and legs. Gradually the woman's lower leg turns purple.

It's frustrating, the woman clicks her tongue. My leg is getting cold. The blood can't circulate. But I'm used to it, you know. It's always like this, endlessly.

I can't take it any longer, this place, I think.

I hope the bus gets here soon.

Checking my watch, I see that the second hand is still moving, jerkily. Like a living thing, stuttering across the white face of the watch, jerkily, moving.

I've been here too long, in this place.

I think, closing my eyes. The moment the thought occurred, I should have been able to go back, to the place I was, in Manazuru.

But I couldn't. There is no sign of the bus. The woman stands, unperturbed, her relatives hanging heavily from her.

LEAVING THE WOMAN standing there, I ran looking for Rei, but the woman blocked my way.

The woman with the mole on her neck.

She gestures with her chin. Looking, I see Rei lying, covered by a summer blanket.

The woman slid in next to Rei, whispered in his ear. Rei opened his eyes, embraced the woman. He did not stop at embracing her, he opened her legs, eased himself in and out.

It was not as bad as when they sat facing each other, talking. I was not surprised.

Bodies are harder to distinguish than feelings.

Gazing at a body, you lose track of whose body it is. Is that Rei, is that really the woman with the mole on her neck, her body, seeing them, it only becomes harder to tell.

It is less remarkable, the act of love, in reality, than when it is imagined. It is sticky, noisy, and however lewd the act may be, in the end, it all comes down to more or less the same thing. However extraordinary the position, however fiercely we hurl ourselves together, it comes to seem that we are only mimicking forms that we have seen before, somewhere.

There is more complexity in our feelings.

In there, no leverage, it is all there. Everything since you came into the world, all you have seen, even the things you believed you had forgotten. It is, how it really is.

And more, what you have never seen, too, the unimaginable, is in there.

Rei presses the woman down, turns her at an angle, rolls her over, keeps going in, and out. It is uninteresting.

"Have you had enough?" I hear a voice, it is the woman from Manazuru.

"I don't feel angry," I tell her. Always turning to her for help.

"It's been a long time."

"Even though I still love him."

"Even though you forgot him, ages ago?"

I never forgot Rei, I tell the woman, and she snickers.

You forgot. You don't come to Manazuru for Rei, it's for yourself.

The woman moans. The one loving Rei. It is a lovely, dirty gasp. Did I cry out like that? Rei keeps moving, saying nothing, intent.

I don't recognize this man, I think.

See, what did I tell you, you've forgotten him. Again the woman snickers.

All at once, the herons take flight. Rei and the woman glance up, startled by the commotion of their wings. They remain joined. I am not even interested, I think again.

I HAVE THE sense, lately, of something catching at the base of my throat, at the place where you feel it when you swallow.

The bus came, and I have gotten on. The woman sits beside me. The field recedes into the distance. Rei and the woman with a mole on her neck remain entangled. Soon, I can no longer see the forms, like shadows, wavering in the dusk.

The sky is dark. The houses, the stores, are all decaying. We are past the rows of buildings, driving through the forest. The woman and I are the only passengers. An oily smell rises from the floor of the bus.

The woman presses her nose against the window, gazes out at the scenery. Just like a child. I think, and suddenly she assumes Momo's form.

"No, not that," I say, and she returns.

"Soft on your daughter, aren't you."

"Is it true? Could I have forgotten Rei?" I mutter, without replying. I feel my attachment, my love, they overflow in me, but maybe, could it be, that those feelings were not for him?

"It doesn't matter, does it?" the woman says.

Am I dying, I wonder? I mutter, again, touching my throat. Is it because I am close to death, that I come, so often, to Manazuru?

"Manazuru isn't a deathbed," the woman snaps, still gazing out the window.

I'm sorry, I say quietly, and she lets go of her anger. Once again, she focuses on the scenery. The bus drives on through the great woods, as the woman calls the protected forest. See, look, that's where I used to gather firewood. And in there, I was with a man for the first time. Over there is where I had the children. That's where they buried me, after I died. And there, there isn't anything there, but I liked it, very much.

Pointing, cheerful, she gives me the tour.

Is it too late, for me to go back? I ask the woman.

No, no. You have a place there, to be.

A place, to be?

It's only when you can't be there, any longer, that you can't get back.

So Rei, I guess, couldn't be?

Maybe. That has nothing to do with me, she says bluntly, and begins, again, to point out the sights. I lived over there. And up there, that's where I collapsed. That's where I stayed, after I got better. That's the place I grew old in. That's the place where I was born.

The bus slows. Each time the woman points, the place shimmers, dully. It's very beautiful, isn't it? I say, pressing my cheek against hers. Yes, it is, she replies.

Rays of light stream down on the forest, from above. There is no trace of the rain that was falling. I want to be with Momo, I think.

I don't want to die, I think, strongly.

I would pity her, if I died. She may have gone away from me, but she would cry if I died. Mother, too, would cry.

Something hard, foreign, hangs in my throat. Pain seizes my chest. The bus drives on, the woman, cheerful, keeps giving me the tour.

FINALLY, THE BUS stopped.

I got out, found myself at the tip of the peninsula.

I came here once. The white building, the restaurant that crumbled, then appeared again, after I stopped for coffee, has utterly decayed, leaving no trace of what it was.

The woman sets off ahead of me, down the stairway that leads from the cape to the shore. From time to time, the stairway breaks off, a sloping concrete walkway appears. A little later, the walkway becomes a stairway again.

There is no wind. The tide is out, the reef that leads out to the huge rock formation in the offing stands exposed.

"Do you want to go out?" the woman asks.

She leads me by the hand, leaping from rock to rock. The rock soars up, too steep to climb. We walk back, gaze out at the horizon from the shore. We keep watching until the sun has set.

"Have you had enough?" the woman asks.

Yes, I reply, like a child to her mother.

Yes. This time, I can go back, really.

"It's best that way." The woman says gently, then sets off ahead of me, climbing the stairs. Her legs are so thin. I want to cling to her, fiercely, the way that child clung to her knees.

"I feel lonely," I say.

"You feel lonely, but it can't be helped."

"I know, but still, this loneliness."

Go on, the woman says, shooing me onto the bus. When I look back, she is waving.

The bus goes, once more, through the forest, and descends the hill. At the bottom of the hill is the town. It will not be in that state of decay, anymore, I know. Lights will be burning, brightly, in the houses, and in the stores.

Sensing a presence, I looked over, and Seiji was there.

"Seiji!" I called.

"Seiji!" A second time.

Seiji turned to face me, an inscrutable expression on his face. His lips parted, and he spoke. I couldn't make out what it was he said.

Then Seiji vanished, we entered the town. The windows of all the houses, all the way down to the sea, brimmed with light, white and yellow. I got off at the last stop, Manazuru Station, and bought a train ticket. It's cheaper to buy a ticket for the reserved Green Car if you get it at the window, did you know that, not on the train? A group of women stood chatting by the ticket gate. The train pulled in, stirring up the air. Turning back, I watched two herons flying toward the mountains, deep in the peninsula. Flying together, white wings dissolving into the darkness.

Ma-na-zu-ru. I whisper, to see how it feels. I feel myself missing it. Here, in Manazuru, I begin to miss Manazuru. *Ma-na-zu-ru.* The pain comes again, in my chest.

eight

"I'LL BE SEVENTEEN soon," Momo says.

So Momo is sixteen.

I had stopped keeping track of my daughter's age. When was the last time I counted, calculated how old she was, in years, in months? One year and eleven months. Two years and eight months. Three years and two months.

Rei and I met when I was twenty-six. Ten years older than Momo is now.

After Rei disappeared, I stopped heeding the passing, the piling up, of time.

"Sure goes fast, doesn't it?" I said, and Momo laughed.

"It's not so fast."

"So, is it slow, then?" Mother asks.

"No, it isn't slow, either. It's just right."

"Ah, just right. The way it should be, I see," Mother says, pleased. "I may have felt that way, too, once, I think. Nowadays, it all seems to go by so fast."

We are sewing, the three of us. Momo is making a bag that will match her friend's. Mother is embroidering dishcloths. I am making a sock for plastic bags, from a design in a magazine.

"That's cute, huh, doing it with felt like that?" Momo says.

When you fold plastic bags and put them in the drawer, pile them in feathery layers, down at the bottom, below the sheets of white, particles of dust accumulate. The almost invisible film of dust that clings to each bag gradually settles, gathers at the bottom, hardens.

"I love it how the bags at supermarkets rustle."

Momo is talkative today. She moves her mouth correctly, before long there will be no trace, anymore, of the shades of her childhood, it is happening to her, too, I can see it.

We have positioned our chairs at the points of an invisible triangle, and we sit facing each other, enclosing an empty space. Momo swings her legs. Mother kneels on the chair with her feet tucked under her butt. I draw light-purple embroidery thread through light-brown felt.

"What do you want for your seventeenth birthday?" I ask.

Hmm, she says, aloud, almost in a whisper, almost asking.

These snaps sure are tricky. It's hard to know where to put them, she grumbles, soon. Just then, she pricks her finger on the needle, frowns. She lifts it to her mouth, and sucks.

"I'm having a hard time thinking what I want," she tells me, speaking through her fingers, her soft lips still sucking.

Make it something easy, Mother laughs. She knots the thread, cuts it. The dashes of thread, embroidered on the dishcloth, are a very deep indigo.

The color shines against the faded white of the well-used strip of cloth.

"REI HAS A mortuary tablet now. I'm thinking of going to pay my respects," I inform Seiji.

We made an appointment to meet, since I have completed a draft of the novel he requested. Shall I read it now? Or later, when we're not together? Seiji asked, and I said, Now.

From time to time, the rustle of a page being turned rose, like a bubble, through the hum of the café. Seiji's eyes looked very calm. He read on, turning back, every so often, to reread a passage. He did not skip ahead, from the passage he reread, to the place he had reached, he kept going, reading it all again, at the same speed.

"It's an interesting story, the way it's gradated," Seiji said, coming to the end, after taking a sip from his drink.

"You think so?"

"It feels bright, but indistinct. You glimpse something, in the shadows."

"Is that a compliment? Or are you saying it's bad?" I laugh.

"I'm not sure." Seiji laughs, too.

It wasn't important, how the novel was, now that I had finished writing it. What mattered, what agitated me, was being here, with Seiji.

And so, at a loss for what to say, I tell him about the tablet. Seiji glances up. We are sitting across from each other, and yet, until this moment, I have been unable to look him in the face. He glanced up so quickly, our eyes met before I could look away.

"Perhaps I'll come along," he says, all at once.

"What?"

"It's that town, on the Inland Sea, right?"

Come to think of it, he had said he wanted to visit it sometime. That town on the hillside, where the light is pale.

"Together?" I ask.

"You don't want that?"

Even though he has gone away? Seiji curls his slender fingers around the handle of his cup. Lifts it to his mouth. I gaze at his exposed neck. I want to touch it, but I can't.

"Okay. Let's go, together," I tell him.

The cup settled into the saucer with a click.

THE AIRPORT WAS wide and white.

Planes took off, swanlike. Gliding slowly into the distance.

Seiji carried a large bag.

"That's not much luggage," he said.

My black bag, even smaller than a briefcase, contains a change of underwear and a linen handkerchief. The handkerchief was one Rei had used. Hardly anything of his is left. I disposed of his belongings five years after he disappeared. After ten years, I let go of most of what I could not bear to throw away before. Now, there is only his diary and a few small mementos.

As we slid into our seats, I caught a faint whiff of Seiji. Then it was gone.

"It's so cold," I said, and he took a blanket down from the overhead bin, and gave it to me. I opened it, spread it across my lap. Still cold, I gathered it, put it around my shoulders.

"Are you really that cold?" Seiji said, surprised.

I shut my eyes, reeled my feelings down, inside, to keep the sense of his voice from fading. Before long we took off, leveled out. I returned the blanket to my lap, gazed up at Seiji's face. He is right beside me, yet he is distant. Only, he is closer than when I cannot see him.

"Do you have any plans, while we're there?" I ask.

"There's a person I want to meet."

"What about dinner?"

"I thought we could go out together."

Suddenly, the sounds in my ear were sucked out, opened outward.

"My ears just popped."

"Mine did, too, a moment ago."

We smile at each other. Seiji sneezes quietly. To think we were together so long. It makes me sad. The feelings I have reeled in seep out. I touch Seiji's hand.

"Ah," Seiji says, squeezing back, barely.

Gradually, my cold hand warms. The flight attendant comes, offering drinks, asking what we would like. Coffee, Seiji says, letting go of my hand. Coffee, I say, the same.

We finished our coffee, and then, until we landed, Seiji read.

I GOT A little lost.

You go up the narrow lane between the houses, go down a little, then go up a little higher, and you come to a shrine, I thought.

Unable to find it, I retraced my steps, but I found myself on a different street. I went over a little, started climbing again, but the road never ended.

I thought I had reached the end, but there was a stairway, I climbed that, and then, at last, I found myself in a small park.

An old woman sat on the stairs. Her cane on the ground, she gazed at the park.

"Do you live around here?" I asked.

"Yes, I do," the old woman replied.

"Do you know the street numbers, in this area?"

The street numbers, no, I can't say I do. I wasn't born here. I moved here five years ago, from Tokyo. My son was transferred, you see. I used to live by myself, but he said he would worry, my son. It's awfully hilly here, though, this town, for an old woman.

The ocean sparkles. The color of the ocean is different here, from Manazuru.

For some time, I sat beside the old woman. Something came, very thin. I wasn't sure if it was a woman or a man, or even an adult, or a child. The old woman took a small tin from her pocket, and opened it. Inside, there were white, powdery drops. Would you like one? she asked, holding it out, and I accepted one, in my palm. It tasted like mint.

"Warm, isn't it?"

"Yes. It will be April tomorrow, you know."

The old woman stood, brushed the dust from the seat of her pants. I picked up her cane and handed it to her. A cat strode out from a gap between two houses. A black cat. The old woman waved her cane, shooing it away. The cat lingered, unperturbed.

Scat, the woman hissed. Spit flew. The cat leapt, ran down the hill.

WHEN I FINALLY found Rei's old house, the trees in the garden were rampant.

It's such trouble to have the gardener come, Rei's father said slowly, following my gaze.

It was a small altar. I lay the handkerchief beside Rei's photograph, held a stick of incense to the candle Rei's father had lit, fanned it gently with my hand until a line of smoke rose.

I kneeled, my feet beneath me, praying earnestly, then slid slowly back, away from the altar. I had never seen the photograph of Rei. A picture, I thought, from before we married, before his cheeks had completely lost the fullness of youth.

In the room with the altar, in the opposite corner, was a low table. Three peach branches were arranged in a vase; dolls, the lord, the lady, their retainers, stood in a glass box.

"Are they Saki's?" I asked, calling Rei's sister by her name.

"No, they were my wife's, from before we were married. They were packed away for a long time, but a few years ago I took them out, and it made the room, with the altar, seem a little brighter, like light, shining in. They used to say that when a family leaves its dolls out on display all year round, its daughters will never find a husband, but there are no women left in this house."

I went over, looked closely at them. The lord and lady were a size bigger than the various members of their retinue. Two of the three women attendants were standing, holding faded golden sake servers in their hands, one with a long handle, another with a handle shaped like a hook. Five musicians sat a step down on the stand, one played a flute, two held small hand drums. Another had a fan, the last held a stick, poised, ready to strike a larger drum. The two trees, orange and flowering cherry, stood at each end of the line formed by the three footmen. The footman in the middle held a platform with lacquered shoes on it. The dolls' faces were all painted white, they had beads, set into the porcelain, for eyes.

"They have such lovely features."

"They remind me, a little, of my wife."

A long time ago, they showed me a picture of Rei, as a child. I remembered that face, the plump cheeks, the hair cut straight across the front, hanging down on either side, like a girl's. Yeah, people used to think I was a girl, Rei muttered.

"Rei looked more like her, my wife, than Saki did."

What ever became of that album, of Rei's pictures? Could he have taken it with him when he disappeared? Headed for some place I did not know, carrying old light?

"I'm so sorry," Rei's father said, bowing until his head touched the tatami.

Please, you don't need to say that. I'm the one who should apologize, I told him, and he raised his face, looked me straight in the eye.

Once again, for a second, something came, thin. It went away. There was a design painted in fine crimson lines on the paper panels of the lanterns flanking the lord and lady. Scattering blossoms, it seemed, but it was like the tiny fire that smolders, always, at the core of the things that come and follow, and in the dimness of the room, I could not tell for sure what it was.

The footmen at either end, one with an umbrella, one with a rain hat, each item wrapped in cloth, affixed to a long pole, pursed their lips, their gazes fixed. All the dolls looked alike. The retainers, the lady, the lord, everyone tidily arranged in a single box, standing, or seated, in silence. I will never see Rei again. It is this knowledge that I need, this recognition. That is why I have come.

When I closed my eyes, the dolls' white faces were still there, deep inside.

I RETURNED TO the hotel, not far from the station, removed my shoes, lay on the bed.

I tried Seiji's cell phone, but I couldn't get through. I fell asleep. In a dream, I saw the old woman I had met earlier. She was sitting in the same posture, on the stairs.

The landscape was not sketchy, as it is in dreams, the hill and the houses and the ocean, far below, were all distinct and clear, all in proper perspective.

"Where are you going, now?" I asked.

"I want to go back."

"Where?"

"Back where I was."

"Is that where Rei went, back where he was?"

"I can't say, I'm afraid, not knowing him."

Nothing in our exchange was out of place, though it was a dream. It was clear. I am trying to make myself see what was clear already. I thought, knowing I was dreaming, in my dream.

My cell phone rang. I reached for it, but it was too far. I was mired in my sleep.

The phone rang a long time. The second it stopped, my eyes opened. Quickly, I retrieved the list of my missed calls. Seiji's name did not appear. Home, it said.

"Grandma has a fever," Momo said, right away, when I called back.

"How high?"

"102."

"Is she very sick?"

"No, she's fine."

I heard Mother speaking in the background. Now, didn't I tell you there's no need to call? I've already been to the doctor. Yes, she sounds the same as always. I smiled, and Momo was angry. C'mon Mom, show some concern!

Oh, Momo, still a child, after all, I almost said, but didn't. Thank you for taking care of her, I said, gravely. I feel as if I have shaken completely free of Rei's shadow. Odd, when the two of them look so much alike, like all the dolls. Rei and Momo are barely connected.

"Take good care of her, okay? Call if you need me," I said gently, and hung up. There is something here, following. It is soft. When my mood is gentle, they are gentle. Maybe, here, in this place, I will be able to let go of Seiji, too.

No sooner had I relaxed, than the thing that had come changed, completely. It was cold, frightening. It is so hard to let go. Looking down, I dialed Seiji's number again.

I REACHED OUT with my chopsticks to take a bite of scallion salad, dressed in vinegar and miso, and all of a sudden the woman came.

It was the first time since I left Manazuru.

"The house was very quiet," I told Seiji.

"You seem, sort of, different," Seiji said quietly, without looking at my face, his eyes fixed on the space where the woman stood.

If I'm different, will you come back again? I wanted to ask. But there is no point in asking. Words are seldom a guarantee.

Soon, this woman, who comes, will go away. I could sense it coming. Coming, not from what I knew, but from the woman herself, directly. It's true, isn't it, it really is, they all go.

After dinner, we walked from the restaurant, my shoulder touching Seiji's. Not because I missed him, but because it was a passing thing. This man I had been with, so long. Once you have let go, he is only passing. It was the same, I am sure, for Seiji.

I invited him up to my room. It's okay, my body doesn't desire you, I said, and he laughed. But I desire your body, I think.

"Chilly, isn't it?" I said, and Seiji nodded.

"I love you," I said, and again he nodded.

Even loving him, even if it is only passing, he has gone. Loving is not enough of a reason to be together. I let Seiji hold the weight of my body. He holds me. I hold him back. If only, just like that, the fracture between us would dissolve, disappear. But we can only be, the two of us, tied to the other.

"Where will you go, when you go back?" I ask.

"Back where I was." He gives the same answer the old woman gave, in my dream.

"Quiet, isn't it?"

"Yes, it's quiet."

It is the same quietness as in Rei's house. The trees in the garden cast shadows on the paper-paneled walls in the room with the altar. The thin thing that came retreated, then came back. Finally, it was drawn into the glass box, with the dolls. The Ministers of the Right and Left carried quivers full of arrows on their backs, the feathers spread, lovely, like fans.

I could hear the beating of Seiji's heart. Or perhaps it was my own heart beating. Coming together, in this room, they were the same thing. Apart, separate, and yet the same.

The sense of its passing grows. My fingertips look very white.

WE FELL ASLEEP holding hands.

Our bodies were not touching, only our hands were linked. If only Seiji had been my son. Or my father. A brother, older, or younger, I thought, as I fell asleep.

When I awoke, the room was filled with light, and we were no longer holding hands. Seiji rolled over in his sleep. It is hard to be sad in the morning. Sadness disperses, purged by the light.

"Good morning," I say, poking Seiji's nose.

Groaning softly, Seiji opens his eyes. I shift my body, display-ing the valley between my breasts. Realize what a waste it is to leave me, I pray, showing him. He is groggy.

"What time is it?" he asks.

"Eight."

"Time for breakfast, huh?" Seiji says, like a child. He has not yet settled, fully, into Seiji.

"Idiot," I say, poking his nose again.

"I'm not an idiot." He is still childish.

If only I could mold him, before he settles, into a form that is right for me.

Seiji gets out of bed, goes into the bathroom. The gush of running water leads straight to the rush of the shower. When Seiji walks out the bathroom door, he is himself again. Glancing at me where I lie, he takes his clothes from the closet, and briskly dresses.

"I'd like you to rewrite part of your novel," Seiji says, leisurely, when he is fully dressed, having settled onto the sofa.

"Which part?" I ask.

"The middle, just a bit."

I had thought of him when I wrote. Sometimes, it was so sad I had to stop. I thought that when I finished it, I would have done, too, with the wavering of my feelings, but there was no relief. The scene with the love letter he faxes her, where she touches it with wet hands, and the writing blurs? Is that the part you mean, the little bit, in the middle?

"No, that's not it."

The blurred love letter, that was lovely, Seiji says, looking directly at me. I walk over and sit down beside him on the sofa. The woman follows. She is only a trace. Soon, I know, she will have gone away, completely.

"Let's get together, sometime, again?" I whisper into his ear. Seiji smiles.

"Sometime, some, distant time," I repeat.

The woman vanished. She will never come again. Through the window of this hotel near the Inland Sea, I can see a small scrap of water. It glitters brilliantly.

Sadness returns, a little. Even though it had dispersed, into the light.

This, too, probably, is only a trace. I smile back at Seiji, close my eyes.

WE PRESSED OUR lips together for some time.

Then, slowly, neither of us taking the lead, we parted.

The places that have separated begin to dry the soonest. It is like lifting a scab before it is ready. At first, it oozes, glistening, and then, before you know it, it is half dry.

Almost immediately after I felt our lips had parted, I was back in Tokyo. I remember, very clearly, sitting side by side in the plane on the way back, and the moment when we waved goodbye in Shinagawa, but everything in between has been swept away.

Momo leafs through her textbooks. She is writing her name in the textbooks for the next grade. Ya-na-gi-mo-to Mo-mo. Why are you writing it all in *hiragana*? I ask, and she tells me, grinning, My name doesn't look good in *kanji*.

"I'm going to file to have him declared disappeared."

The words fall easily from my mouth.

Even though, all this time, I couldn't make up my mind. Even though, all this time, it kept oozing, it never dried.

"Oh my." Mother looks up. Momo is starting to write her name in a notebook. She keeps her head down.

"How were things, there, at Mr. Yanagimoto's house?" Mother asks.

"Very quiet."

This time, it is Mother who looks down. All of a sudden, as though her neck has snapped, her head drops. I peer at her, puzzled. She has fallen asleep.

"Grandma starts napping sometimes, lately," Momo tells me.

She sits in the chair, back rigid, only her head bent, eyes shut.

"Get up." I shake Mother.

"Don't do that, she'll wake up in a second." Momo cocks her head. "Just let her sleep."

Mother opens her eyes a crack. She flicks her hand, as if she is shooing a small insect away, and then, all of a sudden, her eyes are wide open.

"Are you all right?" I ask, and she looks confused.

"Yes, why?" she asks back.

The sun dims, and then the bright rays return. The light illuminates all three of us, from our faces to our shoulders. When we bend, the light rings our foreheads, like crowns. Three women of different age, sharing the same blood, wearing the same crown.

THE PROCESS WAS not terribly complicated. I visited the police station and requested the forms, ordered a copy of our family register, prepared a statement, made a trip to family court, paid a few thousand yen.

"We issue a public announcement, then wait six months," they told me.

In six months, he would be declared dead. I remembered that women are not allowed to remarry for six months after a divorce. There is something peculiar, I always think, about the number six.

When I got home, Mother asked about the procedure. I explained, as if I were explaining the plot of a movie I had seen.

"It seems too easy," she said, an infant's look of wonder on her face.

Evening was approaching, but the sun was bright. The blossoms of the flowering cherries had long since scattered, new leaves covered the branches. I don't like this season, your body can't get settled, Mother grumbled, looking her age again. She touches the hair on her temples, now flecked everywhere with white.

"Where's Momo?" Mother asks, as if the thought has just occurred to her.

School, I reply, and again she raises a hand to her temples. Mom, don't die, please? I think, lightly, as if I am tossing her a ball. Was it always so bright in this house? There are spots, here and there, in the living room, that shine.

Momo picked the dandelions in the glass mug. They open wide, gathering in the light. The dinner table; the chairs, pressed up against the table because they are empty now; the floor the chair legs rest upon; Momo's slippers, left there on the floor; the fine coating of dust on the slippers; the white streaks in Mother's hair as she dusts; the hands, puffy from working in water, that reach up occasionally to touch the hair; the wrinkly arms which the hands are connected to; the wrinkles in her sleeves, rolled up to her elbows—everything shines.

"It's so bright," I said, and Mother smiled.

"Things you've lost turn up on days like this, you know."

Do you think we'll find something? I asked, and she smiled again.

I squinted, without saying anything.

You boil the agar until it dissolves, Mother says.

Wow, agar comes in sticks, huh? Momo laughs.

It's been soaking for about two hours, so all you have to do now is give it a good washing, picking it over, in case there are any little stones.

Momo washes the sticks of agar in a bowl of water, squeezing them. Grandma, is this enough? Rei is present in her profile. Her nose. The edges of her mouth, when she smiles.

She shreds the agar, dropping it into the water, over a low flame. See, the water is starting to get gelatinous. Gelatinous? What does that mean? Like jelly, gooey, but thinner.

The voices that fill this house, women's voices, like three sparrows chirping, are pliant. They do not reach very far, but they never go away.

Then add sugar and milk to the pot, finally toss in the almond essence. Pour it all into a low, square dish, let it cool. Momo has grown a little, again. How warm your hands are, Mother says. So warm, and the water just rolls right off.

The soft, white almond pudding is hardening, now, in its dish. Things made with agar firm up even if you don't refrigerate them, Mother tells Momo. Let's put it in, though, it tastes better cold, Momo says. These hands, handling food, deeply wrinkled, smooth, skin beginning to loosen, touching each other, moving apart, overlapping.

Nothing comes, anymore, to follow.

The space around my body is wide open, slightly cool.

A pain seizes my chest, but quickly goes. I have grown accustomed to this pain. I will walk on, from here, through a dim place, growing accustomed. Beyond all the dimness, perhaps, something like the light that shines into this house will appear, again.

I REWROTE THE parts I had erased, fixed the problems that kept appearing, no matter how many times I read it, found new problems each time I fixed the old ones, more and more, and then, fed up, called Seiji.

"You know a novel is finished when it never ends," he said, suppressing a laugh.

Seiji's voice seeps down, slowly, into my body.

Will I want to meet him? I wondered as I dialed. He was not distant, but he was not, now, very close. I could not see us meeting. Eventually, perhaps, the sound of his name, too, would cease to summon anything in me.

"I'll send it to you, do me a favor and read it again?" I said.

I'll read it. His answer comes, quiet.

Why did Rei go away? Why go to all the trouble, time would have helped him. Time takes everything, and changes it. Time changes everyone.

"You haven't changed at all, have you?"

Seiji seems to have read my thoughts. I am taken aback. I haven't changed?

"The way you speak, it's always been the same."

Always, it feels odd to hear you use that word, I say, and Seiji chuckles. It has been a long time since we met.

"Momo is starting to look like Rei."

I had tried, as much as possible, not to say Rei's name, talking to Seiji. It was easy to say it now that Seiji and I had become so distant.

I remember, clearly, how it felt to love Seiji. And our lips touching, just a little while ago. And the way I devoured him, as if I were crawling into his body, dissolving my feelings in his feelings. But I do not want, any longer, to have it back.

"Children grow up so fast."

I have seen a picture of only one of Seiji's three children. He was a boy, two years younger than Momo, he had just started school. He wore shorts and high socks, his sleeves were too long for his arms. He did not resemble Seiji. He doesn't look like my wife, either. He's in an in-between stage, you can't tell which of us he looks like, Seiji said, smiling.

When I hung up, my mood brightened. Only the gentleness of his voice lingered, swaying, within me, in the feelings I had.

Children, they grow so fast, I said, imitating Seiji, testing how it would feel. Momo used to be so prickly, before, the way she acted, but she has loosened up. She does not say so many things that hurt me.

I remember Momo, last year, in the field that night, with the silhouette beside her. I know that silhouette was Rei. It was thick, but passing.

WHAT WAS IT, there, in Manazuru?

Momo asked.

I don't know. I remember it, and yet I can't remember.

I reply, and she looks as though it is not enough. You were going all the time, you know, leaving me and Grandma here all alone.

I wouldn't say that. I only went three times, alone.

Really? Momo's eyes widen. Is that all? That's funny, somehow I had the impression you were gone for a very, very long time. I guess maybe it wasn't that much, after all.

Momo understands. That I left something there, in Manazuru. Something I left behind me, that will never be back, that these hands of mine will never hold again.

Even when I am alone in a room, and I call out, Hey, into the empty air, nothing comes. Thin or thick, woman or man, nothing.

Empty.

I say, quietly.

And yet, already, something has begun to fill the emptiness. Like the agar, after it has been cleaned, after it has begun to dissolve into the hot water, the agar and the water, translucent in precisely the same manner, and yet with different densities, mixing, becoming gelatinous, that is what it is like, the way, slowly, this something has begun to fill the emptiness.

Sand is not it, exactly, but it is also like sand. The walls of this empty container are rough, and just as agar and water are close, in what they are, the rough walls, and the feeling of sand, call to one another.

Momo, it was Dad, wasn't it, you were with, in the field? I say.

Momo stiffens for a moment, then sighs.

"So, that was Dad?" she asks me.

I do not answer, I only look, steadily, at Momo. Once again, her figure has lost its clarity. How many more times, before she stops growing, will she change?

"So, that was Dad?" she asks, again.

I keep staring at her, without speaking. Dad scares me, Momo muttered. I was frightened, since I didn't know him. I was curious, because I was scared. So I wanted to go, to follow him.

I shuddered.

I'm glad you didn't go, and follow him, I said, touching her shoulder, and Momo nodded. I hugged her to me, hard. I hugged her, hard, twice.

FAR AWAY, DOWN the road, things are coming.

The bottoms of their jackets billow in the wind, flapping. They walk together, side by side, squinting, looking dazzled, the light that enters their squinting eyes is strong.

Are those their beach shoes, I wonder, noticing that with each step, a little sand drops from the soles of their shoes. The man's angular shoulders do not heave when he walks. The woman's sturdy hips do not sway.

I wave hello, and they wave back.

Today, too, the sun is shining. The voices of people out enjoying the day off echo under the high roof of Tokyo Station's Marunouchi exit, where we have arranged to meet.

"It's quite a trip, getting here by bullet train from Hiroshima."

"That's what you get for being afraid of flying, Saki."

They chatter back and forth, laughing.

"Thanks for coming to see us!" Saki says, bowing slightly. "Even though we're no longer family."

"I'm still a Yanagimoto for the next five months," I say, and Saki smiles.

There is no trace of the extreme, youthful thinness her body had the last time I saw her, when my mother-in-law died; she gazes directly back at me, her eyes wide open, much brighter than Rei's before he vanished, her eyelids clearly defined, like all the Yanagimotos.

"The hotel is a bit of a walk from here," Saki's husband, Ryūzō, says.

"Momo is going to join us later."

The Sunday when they called, out of the blue, to say they would be coming to Tokyo and hoped we could meet, Momo hesitated, saying she had plans. On the other hand, she's Dad's sister, right? she said slowly, feeling the weight of the word "sister" in her mouth.

"Sorry for the short notice, she's always so impulsive," Ryūzō laughs, shoulders shaking.

We have a late lunch at a restaurant in the train station, then return to the wicket to wait for Momo. Saki and Ryūzō are both big eaters. They each eat a breaded pork cutlet, covering it liberally with mustard and sauce, then share an order of beef stew. Each has a heaping mound of rice, consuming it completely, without leaving a single grain.

Suddenly, Momo walks toward us, her expression blooming.

"Aunt Saki?" she says, passing through the gate, running over to us.

"Momo, you look just like my brother," Saki says, without hesitating.

"Do I really?" Momo asks.

Sunday afternoon sunlight streams in from outside the station, almost as far as the gates. The trees, the cars, the buildings, everything shines, brilliantly.

LET'S GO SOMEWHERE with some greenery, Saki said, spreading her tourist map of Tokyo out. Momo peered down at it, curious. There's a place called the Wadakura Fountain Park, Saki said, in a resonant voice, and started walking on ahead.

"So, you've been working all this time?" Ryūzō said, coming up beside me. Momo stayed close to Saki, walked with a bounce in her step.

"I guess you could call it work." It's not a steady income, though. Sometimes things are good, sometimes not. It varies. I'm happy we've been able to get along, somehow.

Ryūzō gave an unhurried nod.

In this way, it goes on.

I think, focusing my gaze on Ryūzō's square jaw.

Wadakura Fountain Park was near a large hotel. Oh, wouldn't you love to stay in a gorgeous hotel like this! Saki said. Can't afford it, Ryūzō replies calmly. I remember the inn that bore the name "Suna," run by a woman and a man, probably mother and son. We get lots of fishermen on weekends, the son had said. The atmosphere must be completely different when all those fishermen are there, having a good time, than when I was there, alone.

"What are my cousins like?" Momo asks.

Oh, they never listen to a word I say. If only we had an adorable child like you! Saki replies enthusiastically. Not likely, not the way we raise them. Besides, they're our children, you can't expect such sensitive children from parents like us. Ryūzō laughs, shoulders rocking.

The sun shines on everything. Momo gazes up at the sky, shading her eyes with her hand. An airplane is flying overhead, leaving a trail of vapor. I can't understand how anyone could not be frightened, that far off the ground, Saki says. It's so beautiful, the plane, it's like a needle, Momo says. You know, Momo looks like those dolls in your father's house, Ryūzō says. I used to take those dolls out and play with them, Saki says. Mom was always getting after me for it.

Momo's hair shines in the sun. Saki's face, Ryūzō's ears, the grass in the park, the water in the fountains, the sky over the horizon, everything shines equally under the sun. I close my eyes, feel my eyelids shining. I call up an image of the Inland Sea. Countless fishing boats bobbing, in the offing, on the warm and waveless sea.

Rei, I know, in some distant time, I'll see you again.

On the dark, agitated surface of the ocean, there in Manazuru, the burning boat gradually sank. Coming from a place of nothing, returning to nothing. I heard Momo's gentle voice off in the distance, and the park filled with light.

about the author

H IROMI KAWAKAMI IS the recipient of the Pascal Short Story
Prize for New Writers and the Akutagawa Prize. Her stories and essays are widely published in Japan, where she taught
biology and is now a member of the Science Fiction Research
Association. She lives in Japan.